HyperLinkz

Fudge Factor

BOOK 2 ROBERT ELMER

WaterBrook
P R E S S

FUDGE FACTOR
PUBLISHED BY WATERBROOK PRESS
2375 Telstar Drive, Suite 160
Colorado Springs, Colorado 80920
A division of Random House, Inc.

Unless noted in *The Hyperlinkz Guide to Safe Surfing,* all Web-site names are fabrications of the author.

ISBN 1-57856-748-3

Published in association with the literary agency of Alive Communications, Inc., 7680 Goddard Street, Suite 200, Colorado Springs, CO 80920.

Library of Congress Cataloging-in-Publication Data
Elmer, Robert.
  Fudge factor / Robert Elmer.—1st ed.
    p. cm.—(HyperLinkz ; #2)
  Summary : During their next exciting adventure inside the Internet, twelve-year-olds Austin and Ashley Webster encounter an assortment of colorful historical figures as they try to make it home to Normal, Illinois.
  ISBN 1-57856-748-3
  1. Internet—Fiction. 2. Christian life—Fiction. 3. Science fiction. I. Title.
PZ7.E4794Fu 2004
[Fic]—dc22   2003025421

Printed in the United States of America
2004—First Edition

10 9 8 7 6 5 4 3 2 1

Contents

Introducing...Fudge Factor

Ashley Webster here. I was asked to tell you how my brother and I got to this point, using two hundred and fifty words or less—kind of like doing a book report for Mr. Little's English class back home in Normal, Illinois. That's where my brother, Austin, and I are from. But thanks to Austin, who was fooling around with a garage-sale digital camera, we were zapped into the Internet. Yes, *into*. Literally. Don't ask me how. I don't think even Austin knows.

At first we were trying to find Applet (also zapped into the Internet), my aunt Jessica's prize-winning beagle. She's worth big bucks, so we were afraid we might have lost her for good. Anyway, we found that we could jump from Web site to Web site by stepping on hyperlinks, sometimes on purpose...and other times not. Along the way we met a lady named Mattie Blankenskrean, who I thought at first was pretty nice. Turns out she wasn't. She was using a handheld computer to wipe out stuff on the Internet that she didn't like, mainly parts of Web sites that talked about God and faith and that showed how normal people could believe in something other than themselves. Long story short, I ended up with her handheld, and Austin and I hyperlinked outta there. We're still stuck on the World Wide Web, but now Ms. Blankenskrean is after *us*. And this story picks up where *Digital Disaster* left off.

That's two hundred and forty-four words. Pretty close, huh?

CHAPTER 1

Road Trip

Ashley Webster would have been the first to tell someone how much fun a road trip could be. Feeling the wind in her hair, seeing new places, meeting new people…

Yeah, but how about inside the trunk of a 1955 Volkswagen bug?

"I'm gonna die," her brother, Austin, groaned when they hit yet another pothole.

Ashley heard a *thunk* that gave her a pretty good idea that Austin's head had bounced up to hit the inside of the hood. They were in the front end of the car, since the engines in the old Beetles were in the back.

"Not yet, you're not." Ashley did her best to hold on. "Let's try yelling again."

"I can hardly breathe, Ashley. My face is crunched against the spare tire. I'm going to pass out."

"Stop it, Austin. Don't panic."

But besides being eleven months older than Ashley, her poor brother was a few pounds heavier and a lot bigger than she was. Plus, the VW's trunk wasn't exactly built to hold two people, even if they were kids.

"Try shouting on three." Ashley tried to shake some feeling into her hands. "One, two..."

THUNK! Another bump. The sharp corner of a suitcase jabbed her in the ribs.

Ouch. "Three," she whimpered.

"Hey! Help!" They both shouted their loudest, but their driver just shifted gears. All they could hear in reply was the whine of the small car's engine, the *whap-whap* of its windshield wipers, and the splash of rain puddles outside.

Oh, and the driver's singing.

Full blast.

And a little off-key.

"At least this is only a Web site," Ashley reminded herself, but that didn't help her feel any better.

"It's real enough," Austin told her. "Be glad you're the skinny one."

"This isn't any more comfy for me than it is for you."

That wasn't quite true, and Ashley knew it. But as the driver belted out his version of "A Mighty Fortress Is Our God," she gave her brother a bit more space by inching closer to the sound.

"You sure you can't reach the glove box?" Austin asked. "Because if you can—"

"Working on it," she snapped as they skidded around another corner. The bad news: A suitcase rolled onto Ashley's back. The good news: Now she could reach a few inches farther.

"Got it!" she whispered. At first the back of the square glove box wouldn't budge, but she wiggled it just a little harder, and...

Pop!

The back fell off. Now all she had to do was push out the door and grab the closest...

Knee?

"Yahhh!" the driver yelled as the Beetle nearly flipped over.

"Ashley!" Austin added to the noise. "You're going to get us killed!"

They screeched to a stop in a hailstorm of gravel. And through the glove-box opening Ashley could now see the face of a wild-eyed man staring in at them.

"So clear you are. Unbelievable."

The guy sounded a little like Arnold Schwarzenegger, but he didn't look like the Austrian movie hunk. Except for the wide eyes, he looked pretty average: sandy haired, slim, twenty-something. And like every other person Ashley had met on the World Wide Web, he was slightly out of focus.

"Sorry to scare you like that." She held out her hand. "I'm Ashley Webster."

"You are an internaut?"

Internaut. That would be like an astronaut, only someone who travels to the Internet.

If he wasn't going to shake her hand, she might as well reel it back in. "Internaut. Right. We're from Normal, Ill—"

"We? There's more than one of you in there?" If this guy's eyes got any wider…

Bam-bam-bam! Austin rapped the inside of the trunk.

"My brother, Austin, is here too," she explained. "We just came from a Web site where the apostle Paul was shipwrecked, and—"

"Ashley!" Her brother interrupted. "Would you stop telling him our life story and just see if he can get us out of here?"

"Okay. Long story short: We hit a link for *Heroes Hall of Fame* or something like that, and here we are in your trunk."

Their driver didn't seem at all famous or heroic. His wrinkled clothes reminded Ashley of the way her dad sometimes looked when he came home from a doctors' convention.

Finally the man seemed to get over his shock and reached in to shake her hand. It tingled at the touch, but Ashley was getting used to the feel of digital people.

"Andy van der Bijl." His last name sounded like "Van-der-bill."

"Pleased to meet you." She did her best to stay polite. "So are you a really famous person?"

"Not exactly. This is a Web site, you know. I'm like an actor. No one is real here, except perhaps you and your brother."

"Okay." Ashley could relate to being an actor. After all, she'd played a few lead roles for the Chiddix Junior High Drama Club. Like Kim MacAfee in *Bye Bye, Birdie* and Nellie Forbush in *South Pacific.* "I know you're not really Andy van der…"

"Van der Bijl." He smiled again, as real as any smile. She liked this man, even if he was digital. "Most people just call me Brother Andrew."

Ashley wasn't quite sure what kind of name Brother Andrew was, but she wanted to be polite and not bug him about getting out of the trunk. "Cool. So right now you're on a road trip somewhere?"

"You could say that." He studied the road ahead after they started up again. "I'm bringing Bibles into East Germany."

"In a Beetle?"

Again the smile. "It's the car God provided. It has a few good hiding places."

Hiding… Ashley was starting to get the picture.

"So you're a Bible smuggler. And this is illegal, right?"

"Following God's law is never illegal." But the smile disappeared as they rounded a curve.

"East German border guard." He hardly moved his lips when he said it. To Ashley's surprise, he slammed the glove-box door in her face.

She pushed it back open.

"Hey, wait a minute. What will happen if they find us?"

"You don't want to know."

Ashley gulped.

Brother Andrew closed the glove box once more, this time with a warning.

"Now, stay quiet. And you'd better pray if you know how."

CHAPTER 2

Cybersmuggler

Being in the trunk of a Volkswagen Beetle wasn't the hard part.

Being in the trunk of a Volkswagen Beetle with her brother's knee in her back wasn't the hard part either.

The hard part was knowing that this was a Web site on the World Wide Web and that they were stuck there. It was like going around and around on the Pirates of the Caribbean ride at Disneyland and not being able to get off. Enough already!

And now there was Brother Andrew's Bible smuggling thing to deal with, which was pretty scary if Ashley went by the tone of the voices just a few feet away. As in "you're busted and we're going to throw you in prison for the rest of your life."

Not to mention that a crazy woman was probably still chasing them, trying to take back her handheld Personal Data Assistant so she could go right on erasing any sign of faith from the World Wide Web.

Of course, Ms. Mattie Blankenskrean probably didn't see it that way. As the chairperson for the Normal Council on Civil Correctness, she would tell you she was simply protecting her community by helping to reshape the Internet into an environmentally responsible, politically inclusive, and religiously neutral setting.

Whatever that meant.

As if that wasn't bad enough, Ms. B had already threatened that she was going to make sure Austin and Ashley never ever got home. Maybe she'd been having a cranky moment, but with her hanging around, things could end up being serious.

"Is the driver going to let us out?" whispered Austin. The way he was crammed into the trunk, he couldn't have seen much and had probably heard even less.

"Shh!" Ashley hissed. "Something's going on. He saw something. He said we should pray."

Judging from all the shouting outside the car, praying was probably a good idea. The yelling seemed to come at them from all sides, as if in stereo.

"Pull over to the side of the road!" someone bellowed.

The voice was enough to send chills up Ashley's spine.

"Did you hear that?" she whispered into her brother's ear. Actually it was probably more like his armpit, but in the dark it was hard to tell. "Does that voice sound familiar to you?"

"I dunno. But I have to get out of here."

"Shh. Not now." Ashley tried to settle him down, but she could tell that his legs had started to quiver. His arm twitched. "Hang in there."

She'd seen stuff like this in the movies. The good guys are hiding from the bad guys, and the bad guys are getting closer and closer. Then when the bad guys are just about to give up the search, somebody sneezes. Never fails.

"Please, Ashley," Austin spoke up again. "If I don't get out of here right now—"

"Passport!" The person outside kept spitting out commands, quick as a machine gun.

Brother Andrew mumbled something pleasant sounding, like "Yes, of course. Here you are."

It was silent for a moment, then the person asked, "Purpose of your visit?"

In WWF wrestling, this chick would have had a name like Commander Amazon or Megaphone Woman. But Ashley knew she was no wrestler. Still, she couldn't believe her ears.

"It's her," she whispered.

"Who?" Austin didn't seem to catch on.

"Ms. Blankenskrean."

"No way. We left her behind at the last Web site, back on the beach with the people from the shipwreck. How could she know where we went? And why would she..."

Yeah, why is she here, stopping a Volkswagen full of illegal Bibles and two internauts?

Ashley tapped the pocket of her jeans; the PDA was still there. Of course, the handheld computer was the reason Ms. B was after them. If she caught them and retrieved her PDA, they'd probably be stuck on this rainy Web site forever, stopping at East German checkpoints for the rest of their lives.

Then again, maybe it wouldn't be so bad. Maybe Brother Andrew would let them ride in the backseat of his VW rather than in the trunk.

"Where are you hiding your contraband?" demanded Ms. Blankenskrean.

"You're free to check anywhere you like."

Oh great. Anywhere? Ashley heard someone opening the side door, probably checking under the seat. She wasn't quite sure what *contraband* meant, but it didn't sound good. It probably meant something illegal, like the Bibles.

"Get ready to run," she whispered to her brother, "as soon as the hood is opened."

The latch opened behind them with a sharp squeak.

"Oh great!" Jessica Mulligan, age twelve, clicked her mouse a couple more times for good measure and flipped her long, blond hair away from her eyes. But the more she clicked, the more sure she was.

"They're gone."

She leaned back in her desk chair and tried to think of what to do next. She hadn't helped anyone by searching the Internet on Austin's laptop in the Websters' garage, and so far the search wasn't going much better on her own computer. Austin and Ashley—and her beagle, Applet—had disappeared into yet another link, and Jessi wasn't sure it was doing any good to follow them around from outside the Internet anyway.

But she'd been so close!

"Jessi!" her mother called from downstairs. "Danielle's here. She wants to know if you want to go shopping with her."

Jessi clicked on a link to a health-food juicer. No luck. She went back to the Web site where she'd last seen Ashley and Austin: *www.paulsjourneys.net.* There *had* to be another way.

"Jessi?" Her friend Danielle knocked lightly on Jessi's bedroom door before stepping inside. "I tried to call, but your phone line's been...oh, you're online."

"Hey." Jessi looked over at her friend and tried to smile, but she couldn't tear her eyes away from the screen for very long.

"Well, I was just thinking..." Danielle hovered by the door. "A bunch of us are going to look at new swimsuits, and I was thinking blah-blah-blah..."

Jessi clicked on another link, something about heroes, and she thought she saw something strange.

"Hello?" Danielle sounded long-distance.

"Oh! Sorry. What did you say?"

"You are so spacey, Jessica. I *said* blah-blah-blah…"

There! Something *had* moved inside a little blue Volkswagen. What a Beetle had to do with heroes, she wasn't sure.

Now Danielle was going on about some cute guy in her science class. Jessi stopped her. "Uh, listen, Dani. I'm really sorry, but I have a bunch of stuff I have to finish here at home today, and I think my mom has chores for me to do too. So you go ahead to the mall, and…and tell everybody I'm sorry. I don't mean to be rude. Can I call you tonight?"

"Whatever." Danielle shrugged and leaned closer. "But what are you *doing* that's so important?"

"Uh…" Jessi wasn't sure how to explain.

A message popped up on her screen. *Your connection has been terminated.*

She knew exactly what had happened. She flew from her room and down the stairs to catch her seven-year-old foster brother holding the kitchen roam phone in his hand. "Colby, how many times have I told you to check before you pick up the phone? You cut me off every time I'm online!"

The expression on Colby's face said *whoops!* "Sorry." He slipped the phone back into its cradle. "I was just—"

"Just remember to ask first next time."

Jessi did an about-face and raced back up the stairs to reconnect. Sure, she felt a twinge of guilt for snapping at Colby, but there was no time to lose. *Oh, but what happened to Danielle?*

"I'd better go, Jess," Danielle let herself out of the room with a wave. "Talk to you tonight."

"Great." Jessi drummed her fingers on the edge of the desk, waiting to reconnect.

Her mother came by in the hallway just then with a load of laundry. "Are you well, girl?" She stopped to feel Jessi's forehead. "You don't want to shop, and you're telling Danielle you have chores?"

But Jessi was already focused on the Beetle again.

"I'm great, Mom. Really."

Maybe she hadn't lost them after all.

CHAPTER 3

Busted

Ashley did her best to get ready for her jack-in-the-box act when she and her brother would pop out of the trunk of a Volkswagen Beetle driven by a Bible smuggler named Brother Andrew.

Yes, she knew he wasn't the *real* Brother Andrew. He was just a digital copy that had been programmed as part of the *www.christianheroes.com* Web site that showed some of the things that happened to Brother Andrew back in 1957.

But knowing it was a Web site didn't help Ashley as she and her brother were about to be discovered by an East German border guard who sounded just like Ms. Blankenskrean. Ashley decided not to stick around for introductions. She had a pretty good idea what she was going to do as the trunk lid opened.

"EEEEEEEEEEE!" Ashley let loose with her best ear zapper. It was worth it to see Ms. B's face—her jaw dropping, her eyes bugging out.

"Whaaaah?" Ms. B lost it. As the hood of the VW popped open, her clipboard flew into the air and her knees noodled. She staggered backward the way most people would if someone jumped, screaming, straight out of a car trunk they'd just opened.

Only Ms. B had certainly changed since the Websters last saw her. Instead of her long skirt and purple and pink flowered blouse, she wore pressed military-style khakis, shiny black knee boots, and a peaked army officer's cap. Her long black hair had been cranked up into a bun underneath the hat, so it didn't fit down quite as snugly as it would on a man, but the effect was nearly the same—as in "don't mess with me."

"Sorry I can't stay and chat," said Ashley as she grabbed her brother's hand and launched out of the open trunk of Brother Andrew's car.

Where to now?

"Oh, my leg is asleep!" Austin fell to the wet pavement, clutching his knee. Actually, it looked to Ashley like it was more than asleep. He'd had some trouble with his left hand when he'd first arrived on the World Wide Web. It had looked mostly see-through, as if it were made of ice—probably because it hadn't been in the shot Aunt Jessi had taken with the camera that had sent them both here. Now the trouble he was having with his hand seemed to have spread to his leg, since it was starting to look the same way. One second it was there, looking fine. And the next second it was fading in and out like a bad cell-phone signal.

"Come on!" Ashley tugged for all she was worth. "It can wake up later."

If there *was* a later. Officer Blankenskrean was catching on in a hurry.

"You!" she screeched and clutched her officer's hat to keep it on her head. "I *knew* you were here somewhere."

The good news: They'd caught this guard off guard. They'd bowled Ms. B over onto her backside and into a ditch.

The bad news: She wasn't going to stay there long.

Their friend in the VW wasn't going to be able to help them, but that wasn't his fault. He stood by the open driver's door with papers in his hand and a look on his face that almost matched Ms. B's shocked expression. Ashley supposed it wasn't every day internauts—people from the Outside—visited the trunk of his virtual VW.

If she and Austin were going to do something, Ashley knew it had to be now. And she knew the best way to get out of a jam like this.

Panic.

No, instead of panicking, Ashley scanned the ground for a

link, any link. This was a Web site after all, and like any site, it had links to other Internet sites. All they had to do was…

"There!" She saw blue letters blinking through the rain-soaked pavement on the other side of a guardhouse with a black-and-white-striped barrier arm that went up and down.

Only problem was, another guard had planted himself between them and the link. And he didn't look ready to smile for a camera anytime soon.

"Ausgang ist verboten," he growled, boots in place. Easy for him to say.

"Sorry." Ashley tried her best smile. "Guess my German isn't so good. What did you say?"

That turned out to be the right question at the right time. A balding gentleman in a black tuxedo strolled around the corner of the guardhouse.

"Mr. FAQ!" Austin grinned at the familiar face. "You have no idea how good it is to see you."

"Ah, but I do, young man." The cyberbutler bowed slightly. "In my line of work, timing is everything."

Whatever his line of work was at the moment. Monday through Friday he answered Frequently Asked Questions, hence the name FAQ. Weekends he hired himself out as a spell checker. And now…

"I believe you asked what this man is saying." Mr. FAQ tipped his head to the side. "I've been summoned by my employer, Online Translators Dotcom, to inform you that the German to English translation is 'Passage is forbidden.' "

"As in 'You can't go there'?" asked Ashley.

"Crudely put"—he nodded—"but more or less accurate. Now, if you have no further translation needs, I must return. We're working on an upgrade to the system."

"Wait a minute!" Ashley stepped forward. "You can't leave yet. Tell him we don't want to hurt anybody. We just want to get to the link so we can find our beagle and be on our way."

"Nice try." Ms. B had almost caught up to them, her shock clearly over.

Ashley looked hopefully at the guard, who stood stone silent as Mr. FAQ delivered the translation. But something cracked at the word *beagle*.

"Das beagle?" A smile crossed the man's face, and he pointed at the blue link.

Never know where you'll find a dog person, thought Ashley.

"Ja, ja. Ein beagle-hund. Kommen Sie her."

"He says—" began Mr. FAQ, but Ashley glanced back at the advancing Ms. Blankenskrean and held up her hand.

"Thanks. I got the gist of it."

With a wink, the guard lifted his rifle to let them by and then lowered it again to block Ms. B. Dog folks stick together.

"Now wait just a minute!" Ms. B slipped into her scolding mode. "You kids can't get far."

Well, they could get far enough. As she placed one foot on the blue words that read *Other Volkswagen Links,* Ashley felt the familiar electrical tingle of Web travel.

"You're making a big mistake, young lady!"

CHAPTER 4

Beetle Mania

At first this new Web site didn't seem like much of a mistake to Austin, no matter Ms. B's warning. Especially not as he watched a line of brand-new, silver Volkswagen convertibles zip by.

"Cool!" He caught a whiff of leather seats and new-car plastic. "Look at that Beetle!"

"Beetle, schmeetle." Ashley frowned and tried to keep her hair from blowing into her face. "This is like standing on the side of a freeway. And we're not here to look at cars."

"I guess not."

"What do you mean, 'you guess not'? Look, Ms. B could be following us, or have you forgotten?"

"I know. But you still have the PDA, don't you?"

Ashley patted her pocket and nodded. Austin looked past the convertibles to another row of the new, rounded Beetles— yellow and blue and bright orange. They were a lot snazzier than the old 1950s Beetle they had just jumped out of. But he and Ashley weren't here to shop. He knew what they had to do: find Applet once and for all—and get home.

In the meantime, though, Austin couldn't help smiling as thousands of white-gloved hand icons flew above their heads like a flock of noisy crows. Each one was steered by somebody on the Outside, and once in a while one would break free from the crowd and double-click on a car.

"Look at that one." He pointed at a nearby convertible. "Somebody out there just changed it from Reflex Silver to Galactic Blue. And now they're adding options."

"Must be a lot of people car shopping today." Ashley was looking up and down the rows of cars as if she were trying to find a bottle of ketchup in a new grocery store.

But what was that sound?

"Do you hear something?" Austin put a hand to his ear. "Sounds like a waterfall."

"Here? I don't think so. Tell you what. You go down that row and see if you can find Applet. I'll go the other way. Don't get run over."

But after walking past about ten rows of whooshing cars, Austin started to hear that roar again. Closer this time, and louder. Voices!

"Take advantage of our incredible deals today!"

And, "With low, low on-the-spot financing and incredible factory-to-dealer incentives, there's never been a better time to buy!"

"We *won't* be undersold!"

A herd of car salespeople came marching his way. Even from a distance, he could hear them yelling about floor models and end-of-the-year closeouts. Two at the front of the group caught sight of Austin at the same time.

Uh-oh.

The group stampeded. The two front-runners elbowed and shoved and tripped each other, but both slid to a stop at his feet.

"So tell me," they echoed as fifty others piled up behind them. "What would it take for you to drive away in one of these beauties today?"

Austin looked at all the rows and rows of beauties slipping by. Mellow Yellow and Sundown Orange and Uni Black. Six-speed manual transmissions and four-cylinder automatics. *Very, very cool.*

He sighed as the sales army held its breath.

"I don't drive yet. Sorry."

Their faces fell at the same instant. One of the guys stared at Austin's hand, then at his leg as it flickered once more to see-through.

"Dude. If you weren't an internaut, I'd say you must have picked up some bad code somewhere."

"Sorry." Austin shrugged, but they all turned away.

"Must be eighteen or older to enter," said one, slurring the words together.

"Void where prohibited," boomed another.

"Not valid in New Jersey, Illinois, or Nebraska," added a third.

That's when a tall woman approached wearing a very expensive-looking fur cape and walking a dog that looked an awful lot like... Applet?

"Ka-CHING," whispered one of the sales army.

"I've got this one," said another.

"My turn!" yelled a third.

And they turned on her like a football squad diving on a loose ball.

Only this wasn't a loose ball. This was Ms. Blankenskrean, dressed in her going-to-the-opera finest and dragging *their* aunt's beagle along for the ride! Talk about nerve.

"Applet!" Austin tried to shout over the crowd, but no one seemed to hear him. At least Ashley had noticed the ruckus and had come running.

"Over there!" Austin tried to work his way through the thicket of salespeople. "It's Ms. B again. And she's got Applet!"

As Ashley followed his lead through the crowd, Ms. B seemed to be soaking up the salespeople's attention, pretending to be their number one customer.

"Heavens, don't you have anything more expensive than that?" she crooned. The herd started to drool as they pulled out their calculators.

"Hey!" yelled Austin. "I think I'm going to get sick!"

Well, that wasn't quite true, but it worked. All the salespeople around them backed off in a hurry. And once again Austin and Ashley stood face-to-face with Ms. Mattie Blankenskrean. The woman actually looked pretty good in pearls.

"I thought perhaps you would thank me for finding your animal," she sneered. "This *is* what you're looking for, isn't it?"

When Applet saw them, she strained forward on her leash and let out a terrific sounding "Ahhh-OOOOO."

Ms. B held her back. "So here's what I propose," she went on. "An even trade. The dog for the handheld."

Ashley looked over at her brother, her hand on her pocket.

"And of course I'll send you home," Ms. B added. It sounded good, but...

Just then Applet lunged to the side, tangling her dognapper's legs in the leash.

"Beast!" Ms. B hollered, hopping on one foot.

"Did you see our financing package?" An especially bold sales guy held out a paper for her to sign. "My manager will probably fire me for this, but—"

"Fire you?" shouted the woman. "I'll fire you. Get away from me, you wolves! Jackals!"

Austin had never seen anyone get so red in the face.

"Hey!" Another salesman stepped up, the one who had noticed Austin's leg. "You can't call us names like that."

"What are you going to do about it? If I had my PDA back, you'd learn a thing or two about…"

Applet seemed not to care about the woman's arguing. She strained on her leash, inching closer and closer to a softly glowing red link.

Austin tried to steer her around it. "Not that way, girl." He took a step nearer just as Applet sniffed at the letters. That was enough.

The poor beagle slipped through the link headfirst. *Svoooop!* went a sucking noise.

"Applet!" Ashley lunged, but it was too late.

"Oh no." Austin reached out too.

Eyes blazing, Ms. B dug in her high heels and, standing over the link, yanked up viciously on the leash. Applet must have been dangling on the other end.

"The PDA," she said coldly, "or I let the beast go!"

Austin squinted at the blinking link, wondering what could possibly be so bad about *Volkswagen History.*

He was about to find out.

CHAPTER 5

Browser War

Ashley thought for sure she was going to die. With each bomb that exploded, the factory rattled even more. At least Austin had the beagle, the all-important Applet. The Websters would be lost forever on the Internet, but they'd have their aunt Jessica's prize-winning dog with them. Wasn't that absolutely terrific?

Ashley peeked out from under the big, oak worktable for just a second.

"What has this…"

BOOM!

"…got to do…"

CRASH!

"…with Volkswagen history?"

Volkswagen History was the link she and Austin had dived through to grab Applet's leash. Getting Applet had worked out fine. But no one had told them anything about dropping into

a war, complete with nonstop howling air-raid sirens, thunk-
ing guns, and the thundering roar of planes overhead. The
planes were so loud that she and Austin could feel the rumbling in their chests. And for some reason, good old Mr. FAQ
wasn't showing up to explain it to them either.

She didn't blame him. A quick look around told her all
they really needed to know: They'd been plunked into the
middle of a large, grimy car factory—or a bomb factory. Take
your pick. You had fireworks inside or outside either way.

And either way it looked to Ashley as if the explosions
didn't matter to the groups of people working on an assembly
line of German Jeeps in one area of the room.

KA-BOOM!

Another close call shook the floor, and shards of broken
glass rained down from above. No problem; keep working.
Ashley buried her head under the table, which seemed the
smart thing to do. The dust made her nose twitch.

The German Jeeps looked like the kind in *Hogan's Heroes*
reruns or old war movies. They were a lot like sheet-metal tool-
sheds on wheels, with front ends that slanted down and spare
tires strapped to the outside. People would come to this site to
learn more about the history of one of the world's most famous
German carmakers.

"I think this is where they first started building Volkswagens, Ashley." Austin held a hand over his head as if to protect himself against flying debris. "If this really is Volkswagen history, then we're in Germany, and this is 1940-something. Probably 1944"—her brother went on, answering her question before she asked it—" 'cause it doesn't look as if they have their rockets quite ready."

Rockets? Austin must have meant the lineup of small rockets on the other side of the room. Most of them were still full of loose wires, and the pieces weren't quite fastened together. These definitely weren't fireworks.

"Well, that's a comforting thought. But if this is 1944, those are American or British planes up there." Ashley jerked a thumb skyward. "And they're not going to give up until this place is a pile of loose bricks."

As if the guys in the planes had heard her, another bomb exploded just outside.

CA-RASH!

Her teeth shook from the explosion, and Ashley half expected that she would have to collect them off the floor. Yet the workers kept on with their jobs, probably thanks to a couple of nasty-looking supervisors carrying nasty-looking sticks. The supervisors strolled from group to group, making sure no one ran away or goofed off. Didn't they know there was a war going on?

A wall calendar displaying a beautiful picture of a Bavarian castle proved it. The months had been torn off to show April 1943.

Austin and Ashley knew they had to get out of there.

"This was not a good link," Ashley yelled into her brother's ear, but neither of them looked too excited about crawling out from under the heavy table. Applet, bless her whiskers, had just about dug a hole into the cement floor to hide.

"It's okay, girl." Austin patted their rescued friend on the head. "We'll get you out of here."

"You know something I don't?" Ashley asked as another window blew in, sending some of the workers scrambling to the floor. As the building around them fell apart, she could see that this place was covered with links shining through the soot-covered cement floor. The question was how to get to one. And this time they had better be more careful about *where* they linked to.

"How about *Back to Volkswagen Home Page*?" Austin wondered out loud as he traced his finger through the thickening dust. Ashley shook her head as hard as she could. *No way. Not back to the showroom and Ms. B. If there's any place worse than here, that would be it.*

"Well, how about *Other Prewar Volkswagens*?"

"You think Ms. B would be there?" she asked.

"I don't think so," Austin shook his head. "But Hitler might be."

"Hitler!" Ashley groaned. "No, no, no. What are you, crazy? Ms. Blankenskrean was bad enough."

"He's the one who got Volkswagens started." Austin knew his history, even including history's worst villains.

Ashley grunted as she shoved a shattered wooden beam to the side, but she stayed where she was—beneath the sort-of safety of the work table. After a couple more minutes, the dust started to settle. She turned her head to listen.

"Is it getting quieter?"

Austin listened too. At last he nodded.

"I think the air raid's over."

But not their trouble.

"Here's one!" Ashley pointed. *Heroes of World War II.* "Only question is, whose heroes?"

Ashley didn't get her answer. At that moment they finally caught the attention of one of the work supervisors, a tall woman with a whip in her hand and a look on her face that said something like "I just bit into the world's most sour, rotten grapefruit." Even from one hundred feet away, Ashley couldn't miss Ms. Blankenskrean's dark expression.

Ashley had no idea where the woman was getting all the

old costumes to wear. Some other Web site? She sure was ready for anything. And there was no mistaking her shrill voice, almost as shrill as her whistle.

"Intruders!" she screamed.

Austin and Ashley looked at each other as Ashley gathered Applet in her arms.

"*Heroes of World War II* will be just fine," Austin told her.

CHAPTER 6

Far from Normal

⌐⊡

"Look at it this way." Austin stared through the window of the tiny shop where the Websters now stood. On the cobblestone street outside, dozens of people rolled by on their bicycles. "At least we didn't keep going back in time."

"That's good?" Ashley set Applet down and looked around. Old clocks of all kinds filled the front room. Several hung on the wall, joining a cheery ticktock chorus of cuckoos and ding-dong chimes. Mantel clocks rested proudly on shelves along with a small assortment of pocket watches and alarm clocks, all keeping their time. But what time? What day? What year?

"Oh!" An older man with a wispy beard jerked his head up and dropped an open pocket watch on the counter. As he did, a small, round magnifying lens attached to his glasses swiveled up and out of the way. "I'm sorry. I didn't notice you come in. I must have"—he blinked his eyes and shook his head ever so slightly, as if brushing away a dream—"I must have dozed off."

Actually, those may not have been his exact words. He sounded Dutch or German, and not a word of it would have made sense to Austin without the translation that appeared in a cartoon-style bubble next to the man's head.

"Cool." Ashley must have seen it too. It was like reading a comic strip.

The old man adjusted his glasses as if to give them a closer look.

"Well, it is February, after all." The words appeared once more. "A sleepy time of year in Holland. A little snow, a little ice, a little sleet..."

Ah, so the link had taken them to Holland.

"Sounds like Normal," Austin told him.

"I assure you it *is* normal," replied the watchmaker.

"Actually"—Ashley stepped in—"my brother didn't mean normal. He meant Normal. The town we're from is Normal."

"I'm happy for you." The Dutchman shook his head in confusion. "Ours is far from it. Nothing is normal here these days."

Austin started to correct him, then changed his mind. *Oh well.* He wondered if the cartoon bubbles were part of Mr. FAQ's online language translator upgrade.

"Father?" A pleasant woman's voice drifted out from the

back room, along with the comic bubble showing her words in English. "Do you need any help?"

"No, thank you, Corrie." He smiled as a friendly looking woman joined them. She wore her graying hair short, and her smile matched the honey of her voice. In a flash Austin knew why the *Heroes of World War II* link had taken him and his sister to this watch shop in Holland.

"You're Corrie ten Boom," whispered Ashley, as if the president of the United States had just stepped into the front room instead of a middle-aged watchmaker's daughter.

The woman stopped short. "Do I know you?" she asked.

They didn't have time to answer. Applet yipped as the front door burst open with a startled jangling of bells. A man in a German officer's uniform stepped in on the heels of two soldiers, their rifles drawn.

Yikes, thought Austin. *Where have we seen this before?*

"Where have you hidden the Jews?" The officer didn't wait for introductions as several more soldiers hurried inside to search the shop and the tiny apartment upstairs.

Miss ten Boom shook her head.

"There must be some mistake," she told the intruders. "We have no Jews here."

Austin knew they did. But he and Ashley could do nothing more than crouch against the wall with Miss ten Boom and her father. He tried not to look while the soldiers tromped like elephants through the narrow apartment. His heart nearly stopped when he noticed what Applet had picked up off the floor.

"What's that?" Ashley asked as Austin snatched the little cap from the dog's mouth.

He knew exactly what it was. A *yarmulke*. A prayer cap that Jewish men wore. Proof of who was hiding in the watchmaker's home. Austin squeezed it tightly in his hand. Even though he knew her story, he was amazed at Corrie ten Boom's bold lie.

"Where is the secret room?" demanded the officer. Maybe he'd been taking lessons from Ms. B.

But Miss ten Boom only shook her head. "Lord Jesus, help me," she whispered.

"What? If you use that name again..."

Austin wiped away a hot tear. He'd seen the movie of Corrie ten Boom's life, but living through it, even on a Web site, was too much to take. Not even the hand of Mr. ten Boom resting on his shoulder helped.

Austin whispered into Ashley's ear, and she carefully handed him the handheld computer.

The officer looked over as Austin fiddled with the device. "You there, boy! What do you have?"

Did Mr. ten Boom know what Austin was trying to do?

Austin wasn't sure, but the kindly watchmaker raised himself up to stand between them and the attackers.

"I hope you make it back to Normal, my internaut friends." He turned to smile at them.

"Thank you," whispered Ashley, linking her arm through Austin's after she'd wrapped Applet's leash around her wrist. "I hope we all do."

This time, instead of the familiar tingling feeling, Austin felt himself pushed backward, as if he had just grabbed on to a moving roller coaster.

Everything went blurry.

Tap-tap-tappity. "Oh." *Backspace-backspace...tap.*

Jessi stared down at the keyboard of her computer, the way her keyboarding teacher always told her not to. "Don't look down, please, Miss Mulligan."

But that was Monday through Friday, and right now she couldn't help it. This was still late Saturday morning, and Austin and Ashley and her beagle were still lost somewhere in cyberspace. Typing their names into the search engine seemed to point her in the right direction at times, but she always seemed to be just one step behind.

"There they are again!" She leaned closer to the screen for a better view of a beagle tail disappearing around a corner. And there! A hand that could have been Ashley's disappeared off the edge of the screen.

The doorbell rang.

"I'll get it!" Colby shot downstairs, and Jessi heard her mother saying, "Oh dear, I'm so sorry you had to come all the way over here, Evelyne. You have? Well, I suppose the phone could have been off the hook. Let me check."

A pause, and then Jessi heard her mom calling upstairs. "Has anyone been on the phone or online for the past hour and a half?"

Jessi heard footsteps coming up the stairs, so she quickly reached over and switched off her modem. *And just when I'd almost caught up with them again!*

"You haven't been online all this time, have you?" Her mother leaned into her room.

By that time Jessica had jumped over onto her bed and was hiding behind an *American Girl* magazine.

"Uh, I'm not now." She tried that one on for size, but her mom wasn't buying. "I guess I was for a while."

Jessi's mom peeked over the top of the magazine. Her eyebrows were wrinkled, which meant she was not happy.

"Your sister's been trying to call here, but the line's been busy. She's been looking for Austin and Ashley. Weren't you with those two earlier today? Do you have any idea where they are?"

Jessi licked her lips. Her mom would never believe the truth.

"I've been wondering where they are myself."

"Hmm." Jessi's mom looked around the room. "Well, you need to stay off the Internet for a while now, at least until your Saturday chores are done. Do you understand?"

Jessi nodded.

CHAPTER 7

Demo Derby

A roller coaster would have been a good way to describe the next few seconds.

Roller coaster times ten.

Ashley could feel the twists and turns, but she couldn't do anything about them—couldn't lean, couldn't steer, couldn't breathe. Her cheeks flapped in the cyberwind, if that's what it was. She couldn't move even her eyeballs.

Ashley was just along for the ride—like her brother, who happened to be driving.

Well, *driving* was really too nice a way to describe it. Tapping commands into a half-broken PDA was nothing like turning the steering wheel of a car, stepping on the gas, or leaning on the brakes.

Unless, of course, you were driving in a demolition derby. *Ka-POW!* And speaking of brakes, some way to stop would be nice.

"Not...my...fault!" Austin seemed to force out the words as his head flopped to the side. At least he had managed to hold on to the handheld on this wild ride. It was their ticket home.

If only they could figure out how to use it.

Zing! Web-site backgrounds cleared, fuzzed, twirled, and whooshed by. Who had put the Internet into a washing-machine spin cycle?

Swoosh! Web-page menus—pull-down lists of things to do on a Web site—tumbled by their heads, sometimes clipping them as they zipped by. Ashley wondered if this was what it was like to be in a tornado with all the debris flying around like crazy.

"Ow!" Ashley tried not to cry out when one of the menus clipped her on the elbow. But no wonder Ms. Blankenskrean was so grouchy. If this was the way she traveled the World Wide Web...

Of course, every hurricane has its eye, and even the worst tornadoes don't last forever. Next thing Ashley knew, she was sitting in the driver's seat of a German-style Jeep.

Not again!

Applet looked happy enough in the passenger seat, an expression on her doggy face that said, "Cool! Are we going for a ride?"

Of course, they wouldn't get far sitting up on an assembly

line without an engine and wheels, surrounded by wide-eyed workers staring at them as if they were aliens.

"Uh...hi." Ashley smiled and waved at the guy who had nearly dropped a windshield on his feet. "Thought we'd drop in for another visit." *Not.* She looked over her shoulder to see what had happened to her brother, then helped Austin get right side up.

"I still don't know how to do it," he mumbled.

"Is there a Back button on that thing?" Ashley whispered out the side of her mouth. "Hit it—quick!"

"That's what got us here in the first place." He tried a few more buttons, but without the screen working, it was like making a stab in the dark.

"How about Forward?" she asked.

"I'm trying, I'm trying."

"Anything! These guys are going to have us for lunch!"

Boom. The Internet roller coaster took off just like before, only this time Ashley and Austin skidded to a stop on a dusty dirt floor and smacked into a clay-brick wall. It reminded Ashley of wiping out last summer when she was water-skiing behind her grandpa's ski boat on Wisconsin's Lake Winnebago.

Skip-skip-skip...thud.

"I'm getting used to it," groaned Austin.

"At least the other way we kind of knew where we were

going." Ashley rubbed her shoulder where she had smacked it against the wall.

"The other way?"

"When we stepped on a link. When it said, Click Here for More Car Choices, we pretty much knew we were going to a Web site with cars."

"I suppose."

"Now it's like we're trying to find a TV channel with our eyes shut, and we're just punching buttons on the remote, the way Dad always does."

Austin nodded as he looked around the small, dark room.

"There's got to be some connection." Ashley got to her knees. "Think…*www-dot-christianheroes-dot-com, Volkswagens, Volkswagen History, Heroes of World War II,* and now this…this *closet.*"

"Well, it's about the same size as the inside of a Volkswagen. Could that be a link?"

"I don't think—"

But Ashley didn't finish. Instead, she froze at the sound of two men's voices coming from the other side of the curtain that hung in front of the closet.

They did not sound friendly.

CHAPTER 8

OT Address

"I told you we can't eat that stuff!" Ashley heard one of the men on the other side of the curtain whisper. "It's not kosher."

"Fine," replied the other. "But you don't know the first thing about being an undercover agent. Agents have to blend in. That's our job. Now let's go back to the table and act like nothing happened."

Maybe Applet heard the part about blending in. She chose that moment to growl softly at the voices. And though Ashley tried to clap a hand over the dog's muzzle, it was too late. The curtain flew open, and two big men stood staring at them.

"Internauts," the shorter of the two men was the first to whisper.

"Really? They look like children to me." A middle-aged woman looked over at them from across the room. Though pretty, she wore a bit too much color around her eyes. Still, her smile was warm, especially when she noticed Applet.

"And they've brought dinner with them, I see." She waved toward a simple plank table set up just off the floor. "I like that. So come in, come in. Don't just stand there staring. You're just in time to eat."

Despite the welcome, Ashley tightened her grip on Applet and backed away. Sure, the beagle had given them more trouble than she was worth, but...

"Er, we couldn't." The taller of the two men shook his head. "The Lord God has commanded us not to eat such things."

"No kidding?" The woman looked as if she could hardly believe it. "You can eat leeks and onions, though, can't you?"

The men looked at each other, and she laughed.

"Forgive me." The tall man bowed slightly to Ashley. "I'm not used to meeting internauts. And our hostess isn't used to entertaining visiting Israelites."

The hostess nodded at them as they finally stepped out of what Ashley decided must be her pantry.

"I'm Rahab," the woman told them. "I run a...a boarding house here in Jericho. Best little inn on the city wall. Let me know if you need anything. I think you'll be better company than I'm used to."

Rahab. The name sounded familiar to Ashley, and she rolled it around in her memory as they all sat down at the low table. Applet wagged her tail, begging as usual.

"I know who you are!" Austin announced with a snap of his fingers. Ashley touched his arm to keep him from saying anything silly.

The taller of the men paused as he chewed his vegetarian meal, and Ashley bit her lip when Austin touched a key on the PDA. Were they off for another roller-coaster ride already?

Instead, a Web address popped up and floated just in front of the chests of the men: *www.OTstory.org.*

"You're spies!" At least Austin had the sense to lower his voice. If someone had been listening down on the street below them, the secret would have been out. "Joshua's spies scouting out Jericho."

The Web address changed to a Bible verse as he spoke. *Joshua 2:1.*

"*Oy vey.*" Spy Number Two hit the side of his head with his open hand. "Is it that obvious?"

"It's written all over you," replied his partner, looking at the words scrolling across the other man's chest. He traced a few letters. "Wait till Joshua sees. Maybe we should get him one of these…uh…Bible-verse things."

And then his face grew serious.

"But if *you* can see this"—he pointed to the scrolling words—"and *I* can see it, what about everyone else in this city?"

That's when the tags came alive with Bible quotes, names,

all that. Just like the footnotes at the bottom of the pages in Bibles that explain everything. If Ashley and Austin had wanted to, they could have sat there all night and read the story of Joshua's spies, how they sneaked into the walled city of Jericho, how Rahab helped them, and...

"This is not good," announced Rahab from where she stood by the window. She ducked to the side. When Ashley got up to see what their hostess meant, she saw it too: People on the street below them were pointing up in their direction while three men with strap-on swords hurried toward them, high on the city wall where Rahab's house was perched.

"Time for you to go!" she hissed. And in less time than it takes to describe, she had shoved the spies up a ladder to hide in her roof garden and grain storage spot. She motioned for Austin and Ashley to sit down again, and she set one of the men's bowls on the floor for Applet. "Eat, eat. Make yourselves look like normal visitors."

Without a word or a knock, the three armed men pushed through Rahab's rickety, wooden front door. They barely glanced at the Websters as Ashley quietly held the dog back.

"Where are they?" The lead soldier pulled out his blade.

"Some leek soup, boys?" Rahab drawled. "There's plenty." She was a good actress.

"I see you made enough for your spy visitors." A second soldier knocked Applet's bowl across the room with his sword.

"Spy visitors?" Rahab looked shocked that he would say such a thing. "What spy visitors? You don't mean those two fellows with funny accents?"

"Don't play games with me, Rahab." By this time the third soldier had finished searching the downstairs.

"No, really. I had absolutely no idea who they were." The way Rahab said it almost made Ashley believe the act. "But listen. They left before dark and can't have gone far. If you follow them down the road, I'm sure you'll be able to catch up to them shortly."

"We'll be back to visit." The first soldier turned at the door.

Rahab shook her head as she waved them out. "I don't think so," she said. "Not anymore."

Ashley watched as the men's torches disappeared into the night, and she pushed away a nagging feeling.

"You just lied to them," she softly told the older woman.

Rahab did not respond right away, first wiping a tear from her eye.

"Perhaps the God of these men will forgive me," she whispered. "If He is as powerful as they say…He knows why I did this."

Ashley nodded, not sure what to say or think. Like Rahab, Corrie ten Boom had also told a lie to protect God's people. If Ashley had been in their place, what would she have done?

Ashley thought suddenly of the dumb little lies that came to her so easily—quick fibs and white lies she sometimes used to make herself look better. Those were definitely not the same thing. Just thinking about them made her cheeks burn.

Meanwhile, Austin kept fiddling with the PDA in the flickering lamplight. "Making some adjustments," he said. It looked as if he had gotten the screen working again—sort of.

"Uh-oh." Austin looked up as *he* flickered too. Was that just the lamp? "I think that may have been the wrong button."

"What are you talking about?" But Ashley thought she knew. *Uh-oh's right.* "Austin?"

"Sorry!" Austin flickered again, and it wasn't from Rahab's lamp. "I'll try to—"

Ashley lunged for her brother. She missed grabbing his arm but knocked the PDA out of his hand. Not on purpose, of course, but at least it saved him from disappearing completely.

If only she hadn't picked up the handheld just in time to fade away herself.

CHAPTER 9

FrankLy Fudge

"Awwwww-stin!" Ashley had a pretty good idea screaming and yelling wouldn't do her much good, but that didn't stop her from doing it. As she flew through a dozen sites headfirst, Ashley held on to the PDA as if it were a life preserver.

Whoosh. Where had her brother programmed this thing to take them? She peeked down at the cracked screen and saw that Austin had typed in a keyword.

Liars.

She dug in her heels as she crash-landed at a cartoon carnival, where little boys were running around eating cotton candy and hollering, totally out of control. She scrambled to her feet behind a merry-go-round. Worse than the boys and the noise was her nose. Was there a reason why it had grown four inches longer, Pinocchio-style?

Next Ashley supposed she'd be greeted by a singing cricket with an umbrella. What was the song Jiminy Cricket sang?

When you wish upon a star...

"This is too weird," she mumbled as she tried to figure out how to work the PDA. *Let's see—a keyboard for people with fingers the size of Barbie dolls. A Forward and a Back button. Erase. Shift. Home. Enter.* If Austin could figure this thing out, well, so could she. *So how about this button? Back sounds just perfect.*

Whoa!

Not quite. Ashley ping-ponged around two more sites until she landed facedown in a third.

"Gross!" Warm, gooey stuff oozed off her eyelids and down her cheeks. At least her nose was back to its normal size. And the sweet, chocolaty aroma reminded her of a candy kitchen. She ran a finger across her cheek and popped it into her mouth.

"Fudge?"

"Actually, *www-dot-FranklyFudgeKitchen-dot-com.*" A man in a white apron stirring a huge copper kettle corrected her. "I'm Frank. I keep up with the latest fudge recipes, tall tales, and fibs."

"Fibs?"

"Prevarications, fabrications, falsehoods," he answered, counting on his fingers and sounding like one of those super-fast announcers at the end of a TV commercial. "Whoppers, untruths, perjury, fiction, deceit, distortions, and..."

He caught his breath.

"Bald-faced lies."

Ten different ways to say the same thing. Ashley wondered what this had to do with the fudge recipes that scrolled down from the ceiling.

Chocolate-almond fudge, German-chocolate fudge, black-walnut fudge, butter-pecan fudge.

Maybe this site isn't so bad after all.

Maple-nut fudge, cookies-'n'-cream fudge, Black-Forest fudge. She took a deep breath.

Peanut-butter fudge, Belgian-chocolate-swirl fudge, cherry-choco fudge.

Have mercy!

Ashley grinned and wiped the fudge from her face while a gloved hand icon dropped from the ceiling and clicked on Frank the fudge guy. Someone Outside wanted to see what was going on here.

"At *www-dot-FranklyFudgeKitchen-dot-com,* we use only the finest ingredients," began the aproned host. A smile crossed his plump face as he stood in front of his steaming kettle. "The darkest, richest cocoas, sweet creamery butter…"

Mmmm. Ashley relaxed and listened to the descriptions. The mixing, the cooking, the cooling, the cutting. Finally a Web site where she could spend a little quality time. After everything she'd been through, what was so bad about that? After all, Ms. Blankenskrean was a long way away.

"Try all the samples you want." Frank held out a plateful, and Ashley gladly helped herself.

"Don't mind if I do."

But a few seconds later, a strange thing began to happen. Probably it was a bad batch, so Ashley decided to be polite and not tell Frank about the weird, bitter taste that had sneaked up on her tongue.

"More?" asked Frank.

"Sure." Anything to cover the yucky taste. This time Ashley inhaled four big pieces of choco-marble fudge. There, that was better.

For about ten seconds. This time the aftertaste nearly scorched her tongue.

"Uh." Ashley hopped around as she pointed to her mouth. "Iz diss how it's supposed to taste?"

He grinned. "I see you've discovered the fudging."

"Fudg-ING?"

"You develop a taste for it." Frank skipped through the kitchen. "The more you fudge, the more you like it."

"Wait a minute." Ashley held up her hands. "Explain to me again what kind of fudge we're talking about here?"

"Like I said before: prevarications, fabrications, falsehoods, whoppers—"

"All right, all right. I think I get it now. So this is like a Sunday-school object lesson, and I'm the bad example?"

"We don't do Sunday school here. This is a fudge kitchen. I'm just being Frank. We do fudging."

"You're not being frank. Fudging is lying. Lying turns bitter. You don't have to hit me in the face with it."

"Looks like you already have been."

Well, not anymore. Ashley grabbed a dishtowel to wipe the bitter fudge off her face. Trouble was, the fudge made her hands a little slippery, and—*whoops!*—the handheld computer sailed from her fingers into a copper fudge kettle.

Plop!

But Frank didn't notice. Bright lights flooded the kitchen, and he lit up.

"Remember, nothing artificial!" he explained to the Web cam—a camera for taking pictures or videos that went straight to the site. "Let me be frank with you. One hundred percent *all*-natural ingredients and *no* artificial flavors."

Ashley edged closer to the kettle, trying hard to remain off camera. If she could reach over and grab the PDA, she'd be out of there. She leaned over a carton marked *artificial cherry substitute* next to a bottle of *artificial vanilla flavoring*. Frankly, this was too much.

The fudge guy stirred his kettle with a big wooden spoon as he went on. "My favorite is this…" His voice slowed as he pulled the dripping PDA out of the mix. "Fudge-flavored computer-shaped treats!"

Yikes! Will it ever work again? Ashley tried to get Austin's attention, but he was caught up in being live on the World Wide Web.

"Have you ever seen anything so lifelike?" he asked. "We're cooking up this tasty treat for the people in your life who love fudge *and* their handhelds. Order your own now. In fact, if you order online, we'll give you a *free*—"

This was Ashley's chance. As Frank gabbed about online ordering, she reached over to the counter where he had set the gooey PDA right next to an open tray of still-hardening fudge. But just as she touched it, Frank reached back once more.

"Let me show you." Frank clamped down on Ashley's hand, which was clamped down on the little computer, which still must have had some life left in it.

Ashley didn't mean to make trouble for Frank, but she pulled at the PDA, and Frank pulled back. A second later they had slipped and were both up to their elbows in the big tray of fresh fudge, looking like two mud wrestlers.

Frank laughed straight at the Web cam as if it were all planned.

Ashley, on the other hand, squeezed the handheld. She felt it vibrate.

"A perfect gift for your friends in Tokyo, where they've got a yen for good fudge!" Frank held up Ashley's hand toward the Web cam.

Ashley squinted her eyes shut as the PDA began to vibrate even harder. The lights started to dim. But she heard no *whoosh* this time, just a bit of a *blop* and a *bzzzit*. It was like a TV remote changing channels. Talk about smooth!

Ashley opened her eyes.

And almost wished she hadn't.

CHAPTER 10

After the Internauts!

"Two points!" Jessica smiled to herself as her wadded-up T-shirt sailed straight into the open laundry-chute door.

"Is that all your laundry, Jessica?" Her mother's voice echoed up the chute from the basement.

"All for now, Mom," she called back down.

"And the rest of the room?"

"Spotless."

Well, it was pretty much spotless. Everything that used to be on the floor had found a new home under her bed or had been stuffed into the corner of her closet. *Perfect.* Jessi hurried back to her real work for the day, hoping to spot a certain beagle.

She scrolled up to the top of the screen to a Search box and typed in *beagle* once more.

Searching..., replied the computer as a dog bone spun.

"Come on, Applet." She tapped her finger against her keyboard. "I know I saw your tail earlier!"

"Jessica?" her mom called from down the hall. "Shouldn't you be thinking about getting Applet ready for the show next week?"

"That's a good idea, Mom."

A great idea—if Jessi could ever find her.

The torches told Ashley it was evening.

How far down to the street was it from her perch on the Jericho city wall? Ashley had forgotten her tape measure at home.

High enough to go splat, she thought as she backed away from the edge. *Fifteen feet, easy.* She tried not to shake. Of course, traveling from a sweet-smelling fudge kitchen back to a dusty Old Testament–history Web site would be a shock to anybody. At least Ashley was still holding the PDA. And even though it was coated with a thick layer of Frankly-Fudge-Kitchen, supreme-Belgian-chocolate-swirl fudge, it had brought her back to where her brother and Applet had been trapped.

And back to Ms. Mattie Blankenskrean, judging by the sound of the voice inside Rahab's small house. Actually, the place was like a wooden tree house, only without the tree. And without the wood. Ashley peeked in through the lone front window, then noticed the people down on the street staring up in her direction.

Maybe they hadn't ever seen a twelve-year-old fudge-dipped girl before. Of course, who could tell in the dark? She waved at a lady with a donkey. *Nothing to worry about, ma'am. Everything's under control—I hope.*

"How many times do I have to tell you?" Ms. B's voice drifted out through the window for all to hear. "This is all *your* fault, and I hold you responsible. Do you hear me, young man? It's *all* your fault!"

"I still don't know what you want me to do about it." Ashley could tell her brother was doing his best to calm things down. That was the same voice he had used when he broke the vase their mom got in Mexico.

"Then let me explain it to you one more time," she told Austin.

By this time a small crowd had gathered down on the street, and they were looking up as if this were prime-time TV. Ashley supposed that without any hockey games in this town, a shoutfest like this was probably the next best thing.

"The instrument is highly valuable, as you know. It's vital to the ongoing work of the Normal Council on Civil Correctness. And your stealing it is highly unethical."

Ashley had to think that one through. *Unethical.* As in

having no ethics. And ethics, of course, are those guidelines that a group of people agree are right.

Ashley couldn't help herself; she started giggling. Ms. B calling *her brother* unethical? Maybe the woman had forgotten everything that had happened in this crazy adventure.

On the other hand, the PDA probably *did* belong to Ms. B, even if she was doing evil things with it.

"Look, my young friend," the woman went on. "These city walls are not about to fall down by themselves, no matter what the fable says."

"If you think the Bible is a fable," argued Austin, "that's where you're wrong."

Ashley pumped her fist, as in *Yeah! You tell her!*

She could hear Ms. B's sigh all the way outside. "If believing that makes you happy, then I'm glad. But on behalf of the NCCC, I'm here to correct that silly story about the Jericho walls miraculously falling down."

"They did fall down, and it's not silly."

The woman laughed. "Certainly that's what this misguided Web site says. But as soon as I get my handheld back, I'll just fix that and be on my way."

What to do? Ms. B clearly wasn't going to let up the attack, so Ashley started planning her own. She looked down at the top edge of the wall. It sure was crumbly. If a girl wasn't careful, she could easily…fall.

Even Ms. B must have heard Ashley's "Whoa!" as she fell. At least she held the PDA tightly to her chest as she tumbled backward, straight into the crowd. And though she might have hoped to fall into a canvas awning, the way people do on TV, this was not TV. She felt every broken basket poking her in the back. She felt every piece of broken pottery, and she felt the dogs that were licking at her fudge-coated arms. She saw every angry face, eyes narrowed at her and mouths yelling at a hundred miles an hour.

Okay, so Ashley didn't understand every word. The on-screen translator wasn't keeping up with the flood of Jericho-speak. But it didn't need to.

First, they must have been calling her lots of names. That would go along with the two-handed waving. Better not to see that translation.

Next, they must have been asking her who was going to pay for all the broken stuff. That would go along with the pointing at the broken things.

And third, they must have been telling her that they were going to call the Jericho police. That would go along with the finger wagging. Like when she heard her mom say, "Wait until your father gets home."

"I'm—" She tried her best to apologize as she tried to find the breath that had been knocked out of her. Did her arms and legs work?

"I'm...down here!" she squeaked at the faces looking down at her from the top of the wall, but all the yelling drowned her out. Oh well. Maybe they wouldn't have understood her anyway.

When the shopkeeper pulled Ashley to her feet, though, she saw Austin. That was good.

She waved.

Austin saw her. That was even better. He waved back.

And Ms. B saw her too. That was not so good. Because the woman headed right for the ladder leading down to the street, crying, "She has it! She has it!"

Oh, right—the PDA. Surrounded by an angry mob, Ashley had nowhere to hide.

CHAPTER 11

Big Pile of Dirt

Down on the street, Austin did his best to put it all together. Ashley had come back…and had dropped in on a shopkeeper's basket display, which hadn't done great things for the baskets. So now Ashley was caught in the middle of a bunch of screaming Jerichites…er…people from Jericho. And Ms. Mattie Blankenskrean was flying down a ladder to reclaim the hand-held computer, now back with his sister. *Yeah, now's definitely a good time to run,* Austin thought as he huffed to catch up with his already-scrambling sister.

"You ungrateful little monster!" screamed Ms. B, who didn't seem to care who heard her. "You come back here with that!"

"I'm surprised…she gets away with…such rude language," Austin panted as he ran interference for his sister through the streets of Jericho, kind of like what a football player does to get through tacklers. If he counted the shopkeeper with the broken baskets and Ms. B, this was very close to being the same thing, only without the football and the TV commentators. In any case, Coach Nelson back home would have been proud. Austin still might not have made the football team, but the coach would have been proud.

"Coming through!" Austin let Applet all the way out on her leash so the dog could run ahead. He'd tied the end to his belt, which might not have been the smartest move of the day, but it worked. They vaulted through a flock of chickens. Think feathers and squawking times two. Ms. B followed just a few steps behind.

But they still had a problem, and it didn't take a rocket scientist to figure it out.

"You can run," hollered Ms. B, "but you have nowhere to hide!"

For once Austin thought the woman might be right. He and Ashley looked right and left, down a narrow alley, past another row of crooked, clay-brick houses. How far *could* they run?

"Here, let me see that thing." Austin held out his hand, and Ashley tossed him the handheld. They followed Applet into a short walkway between two houses. Bad turn. Actually, *walkway* was too nice a word. The smell of rotting kitchen garbage and the growl of a seriously ugly brown dog told them it was nothing more than an alley.

Uh-oh.

Austin glanced down at the PDA for help. He couldn't believe what he saw.

"Ashley, what did you *do* to this thing?" he asked. "It's all covered with—"

"Long story. Let's just find a link—or make that thing work, would you?"

Even though the keys were gooey, Austin punched the Forward button a few times. Nothing. Meanwhile, the alley dog showed its teeth, and the hair on the back of Austin's neck stood on end.

Applet decided this was a good time to do a one-eighty.

"Whoa, back up." Ashley probably figured they would let the alley dog hang on to his bone. She shifted into reverse herself—right into the clawlike grip of Ms. Blankenskrean.

"Let's…take a look…at my PDA, shall we?"

The pauses…were…Ms. B…trying…to catch her breath. Being out of breath did not make her grip any weaker, however.

Austin looked back and forth between his two choices: an angry dog…or an angry woman.

"Now would be a good time to make that thing work," whispered Ashley.

"Give it to me." Ms. B put out her hand, and Ashley did a sideways wiggle out of the one-handed grip and stooped to scoop up Applet.

"Run!" she yelled.

It seemed like a good idea at first, but the alley dog must have thought they were making a move on his leg of lamb. He snarled at them as Ms. B leaped, arms open, to try to keep them from escaping. Of course, that's when the shopkeeper finally caught up with them, shouting and waving the pieces of a broken basket. Add Austin, Ashley, and Applet to the pileup, and...

BAM! Everyone's arms and legs ended up in a spaghetti-like tangle. Even so, Austin did his best to hold on to the PDA. He kept pushing buttons. Something had to work. But...

"Is that your elbow?" He would have been able to sit up fine except for the weight of his sister's shoulders pushing his face into the dirt. Applet tried to get loose, but there was no going anywhere for her either.

"Sorry." Ashley managed to get up.

"Looks like we made it out of there just in time," Austin said, glad to see they'd finally hyperlinked to another site. Their friends from Jericho were nowhere in sight. Except...

"Except where's the handheld?" he asked. He checked the ground all around them. Nothing.

"Oh no." Ashley groaned. "You didn't leave it behind, did you?"

"I thought I had it," he explained, suddenly feeling sick. "But at the last minute it kind of slipped out of my grip."

"Aw, Austin."

"Well, somebody got it covered with fudge. It wasn't exactly easy to hang on to. Besides, we should be able to get it back."

"How?"

"I'm thinking."

As he did, he looked around for the first time.

Weird: The craggy hills in the distance looked almost the same as the ones they had left behind. Instead of a city, though, they found themselves by a flimsy tent, more like a canvas sun shelter, next to a really huge mound of dirt. It could have covered the old city-hall building back in Normal.

Weirder: Off in the distance, a cloud of dust rose from a small group of people who looked as if they were digging into something. Austin swatted at a family of flies that buzzed around his head; already he could feel the sweat trickling down his back. Applet sniffed the air, as if wondering what had happened to the alley dog with the bone.

Weirdest: A bright blue banner—as big as any in a street parade—across the top of their new world told him where they had landed.

"Hmm…*www-dot-ArchaeologyOnline-dot-com,*" Austin read with his head tilted back, taking it all in from left to right. "Your online guide to the world of buried ancient history."

"Sounds like a lot of dust and dirt to me," Ashley frowned.

"This is actually pretty cool," said Austin, ready to check

out some of the links: *New Discoveries, New Digs, Ancient Cities Unearthed…*

"But look, Austin, we don't have time for running off to any links. We have to find the PDA and get out of here, get home."

Don't remind me, he thought.

He knew she was right. And it was his fault for losing the handheld. How had it slipped through his fingers?

"If we could just get the PDA back." He kicked at the dirt.

Ashley poked him quietly with her elbow and pointed to the tent. "Don't look now," she whispered in his ear, "but guess who's just around the corner."

Austin glanced up just in time to see Ms. Mattie Blankenskrean working on her crippled PDA. She'd come here with them after all! And it looked as though her little computer had some life in it yet.

Ms. B saw them, smiled, and waved by holding up her hand and wiggling her fingers. As in "tootle-oo."

"Have a good life, kids," she told them.

And she faded away.

CHAPTER 12

Buried Links

"You can't keep blaming yourself," Ashley told her brother as he paced around the ruins of *www.ArchaeologyOnline.com,* the Web site where the sun was turned up to high and where subscriptions to *Archaeology Online Magazine* were only $16.99 for twelve colorful issues. Ashley watched the obnoxious pop-up ads from the shelter of a yellow-and-white umbrella.

Ka-POP! Another ad popped up in front of her face, creating a bit of a breeze, which was okay.

"But it's all my fault." Austin kicked a rock at where the Jericho wall probably used to stand. "We wouldn't be stuck here if it wasn't for me."

True. But Ashley did her best not to agree with him out loud. They'd already been through it a dozen times since Ms. B had abandoned them. Besides, it hurt to talk. Each breath felt as if it scorched her lungs. And anything else she said would probably sound like whining.

As in "Man, it's hot."

As in "Stupid flies!"

As in "How are we ever going to get home without the PDA?"

Ashley kept her mouth shut and let her brother check out the site.

"Wait a minute. You should see this!" Fifteen minutes later Austin was down on his hands and knees, probably brushing through layers of dirt or looking for broken pieces of pottery.

"Tell me when you find a way home." Ashley didn't move, couldn't move. She felt as if all her strength had disappeared into the dust that rose around her in the waves of heat. She wasn't sure where her tears came from, only that they came, and they probably made tracks down her dusty cheeks. She thought about swimming at Lake Winnebago last summer, about dipping her bare toes into the water off the dock by the state park. Ah, back to real life. Back to Normal...

"Are you all right, Ashley?"

She blinked her eyes open and caught her breath the way people do when someone wakes them up after they've fallen asleep in the car and they discover they've been drooling on the shoulder next to them.

"Wonderful." If she'd been back on the Pinocchio site, her nose would have started growing again.

Austin looked at her sideways as if he didn't believe her.

Smart kid.

"Come on, you'd better get up." He held out his hand. "You don't look so good. Come see what I found."

She only groaned, so he reached down and dragged her to her feet. She felt like a giant Raggedy Ann doll, only without the smile.

A thought struck her. If they couldn't ever get back to the real Lake Winnebago, maybe they could find a Lake Winnebago Web site. Or maybe even Evergreen Lake, which was closer to home. Hey, what about that?

"Over here." Austin walked Ashley over to a small pit on the far side of the dig, where people had been searching for ancient stuff. "Really, you've got to see this."

"It looks like a hole." She was ready to start crying again, but the tears had dried up just like everything else around there. Instead, she watched her brother pick up a hand shovel and start digging.

He grunted as the sweat began to run down his face. "Don't you see?"

Ashley still didn't know what she was supposed to see. But Austin looked pretty excited about his discovery. She decided to be glad for him.

"It's the link we need, Ashley."

"Why under the sand? Why don't we just step on it, like everywhere else?"

"Because of the way this site is built. You only find things here when you dig."

Oh. Whose fabulous idea was that? But even Applet seemed excited, helping with some digging of her own and adding to the clouds of dust that made Ashley choke and turn away.

"I guess this is okay," she admitted at last, "if we want to go to...what's that? *Archaeology in the Movies?*"

She could see the link in the dirt now too. Only this wasn't quite like other links they'd used. Instead of bright blue or red letters appearing just beneath the surface, these were deep down.

"Tell me again why you're so excited about this link." Ashley wiped the sweat from her eyes and blinked away the stinging.

"Oh, come on, Ashley." He dug as if there were buried treasure beneath their feet instead of a hyperlink to who knew where. "Who's the most famous archaeologist in the movies? You know...the guy with the bullwhip and the funny old hat?"

"Oh, I get it, I think. But I still don't see—"

"And what state is next to Indiana?"

"Depends. North, east, south, or west."

"Think Illinois. It should all link together. And when you get to Illinois, what town is right in the middle of the state? The home of Austin and Ashley Webster?"

"You really think we'll be able to get back to Normal by digging down to this link?" she wondered out loud. "With that tiny shovel, we could be here for years."

"You have any better ideas?"

"Let me think about it." Ashley forced a smile.

"Hey, that's my line. I'm the thinker, you're the doer, remember?"

"Well, I'm done doing."

Ashley started to step back away from the dust, but she didn't get the chance. The ground shifted beneath their feet like a jiggling Jell-O mold.

"Did you feel that?" Ashley grabbed her brother as the dirt crumbled then opened to swallow them up.

Well, Jessica had thought it was going to work, but holding a magnifying glass up to the computer screen only showed a weird red-, green-, and blue-dotted rainbow.

"Hmm." She pulled back to squint at the Web-site pictures of ancient digs in Bible places. Solomon's stables. Capernaum. Old Jerusalem. Plenty of strange names, plenty of holes in the ground, and plenty of dust.

"I'm sure I couldn't do that sort of work," she told herself. "Where would I wash my hair?"

She sneezed at the thought of all that dust. Still, she'd seen the dog prints, though only once, and then they'd disappeared. She was convinced they belonged to Applet. And then she had noticed the link to a site called *Archaeology in the Movies*...and one about movie stars.

"Ooo, he's cute." Jessica clicked on the name of one of the stars, forgetting for a moment about her missing relatives. She would probably need to back up to find them.

In a minute...

CHAPTER 13

Indiana Hero

"Well, coming here seemed like a good idea back at the last site." Austin coughed and looked around, trying to figure out where they were. It would take their eyes a few minutes to adjust from the bright bright to the dark dark. At least they were out of the blasting hot sun. His sister ought to be happy about that.

Oh right. His sister!

"You all right?" He touched Ashley's shoulder to make sure. Applet was up and around already, skittering at the rumbling sound that seemed to shake the dirt floor. Austin thought this place sounded a lot like the inside of a subway tunnel, except without the subway.

"If you consider where we've been," she mumbled, "I'm doing great."

Okay, that was closer to the truth than the answer she would usually give in times like this. "Doing great" could mean she was still breathing. She was. "Doing great" could mean all her bones weren't broken after all. They weren't. Or "doing great" could mean she wasn't in the path of a huge, rolling stone ball, and a wide-eyed man in an old-fashioned felt hat wasn't about to run them over.

Two out of three isn't bad, thought Austin.

"Uh-oh. Time to go again!" Ashley snatched up Applet and launched into the air, gymnastics style, to follow the man who had just sped past them. Forget how limp she had looked five minutes ago. Since the elephant-size stone ball was about as large as the tunnel, running was a smart move.

"Are you—" Austin yelled at the man.

"No, I'm not!" The stranger huffed as they pounded through the dark tunnel. "Not who you think I am, anyway."

Come to think of it, this guy had white hair and glasses. Nice looking and everything, but not exactly a movie star. So who were they following?

"On another site, I'm Dr. Robert Braidwood," explained the man, "the University of Chicago archaeologist. My wife and I made a few discoveries in the Middle East. Uncovered an ancient village in Turkey. We had quite a time."

"So you're really not a movie star?" Austin tried not to sound disappointed. Being a famous archaeologist was great and everything, but...

"Sorry to disappoint you," the man told them, as the big

stone was catching up to them. "It think it's some kind of pro-gramming glitch. Short circuit or something. They do tell me I was the *inspiration* for a movie character though—if that helps you any."

Austin wasn't so sure. He *was* sure that about ten steps behind them, the stone was winning the race. Make that eight steps. He started thinking about what happens to cookie dough when it's rolled out for Christmas cookies.

Six steps.

"Tell me again why we're here?" Ashley had a point. Of all the *Archaeology in the Movies* links, they would have to end up in this one. Wouldn't a nice, safe snake-pit scene have been better?

"Like I said"—Austin huffed to keep up…four steps—"it seemed like a good idea at the time."

As they sprinted only two steps ahead of the rolling stone, Austin scanned the rough floor for a link. Hopefully they could find a good one before getting smashed flatter than cookie dough.

"What about down there?" Ashley pointed just ahead of them and panted as she struggled to run faster without drop-ping Applet. Something glittered blue but out of reach. There was no way they could make it.

Sitting out under the desert sun at *www.Archaeology Online.com,* Austin had actually thought maybe this site would lead the way home. Indiana leads to Illinois, which leads to Normal. Simple—or so he'd hoped. Sure, it was a long shot, but a boy could dream.

"In here, kid!" The professor yanked Ashley into a nook in the wall. Austin followed—not a bad move, given that the boulder was about to do its thing.

"UHHHHUP!" Austin pressed his face against the rock, glad to feel his nose flatten because that meant he was still a boy and not a cookie.

The rock whooshed by on its way down the tunnel, brushing past Austin's behind. Time to celebrate? The man who had saved their lives unfolded himself from the hole in the wall and gasped for breath. Ashley still held Applet in her arms.

"Wow. How can we ever—" She tried to thank the guy, but he wasn't going to allow it.

"You don't."

"But you—"

"Forget it. You run through this act a few times, and you figure out a few tricks. Your big problem is getting out of this Web site," he added, "before the next double-click starts the stone rolling all over again."

"Okay." Austin agreed and began to explain his plan, but Professor Braidwood wasn't buying it.

"Nice try." He paced the cave from side to side. "But did

you really expect a link between Indiana and Illinois, just on account of the state names?"

"Well…" So maybe Austin's plan was a little weak, but at least it had gotten them out of the archaeological site.

"Listen, kid." The professor slipped off his glasses. "I'm not supposed to be here, and neither are you. But besides that, your arm looks pretty bad." His eyes narrowed to slits. "Your leg, too."

"My arm?" Austin looked down at himself. With everything that had been going on, he'd almost forgotten. But now it was pretty obvious that the see-through part of his left hand had spread up past his elbow.

"You've got some bad code," said Professor Braidwood. "And it looks like it's spreading."

"But I'm not part of a Web site. I'm real."

"Hey, don't ask me for technical advice," the professor shrugged. "For now you seem digital to me, internaut or no internaut."

"Is this like a disease?"

"I've seen it before. Somebody like me catches what you have, and it's all over. We just slowly disappear. First the arms, then the legs… In fact—"

The man suddenly backed away and wiped his hands on the front of his ripped shirt, as if he could have caught some nasty e-germs.

"In fact," he said again, "I'm not about to catch what you have. I'm outta here. Sorry."

"Wait!" Austin held up his see-through hand, which had gone nearly invisible. *Oops.* "We still have to get out of here."

But the professor had already started down the tunnel. He stopped but didn't turn around.

"All right. But don't tell anybody I told you."

"Told us what?" asked Ashley.

"Behind you...ten paces. I earned my PhD there in '43. Maybe there's something on that link you can use."

"No kidding?" Austin perked up. Sure enough, ten paces behind them, a dark green menu, filled with University of Chicago links, stretched down the side of the cave. The menu listed programs like law and chemistry, staff, history, the campus...

But without the PDA, how could they work the menu? Every link was just out of reach.

"Sorry," the professor shrugged as he jogged off. "Wish I could help, but it's show time again."

Austin thought he heard a distant rumble. *Uh-oh.* The boulder again? Ashley looked up too. They had to reach the link—and fast.

"I can reach it, Austin." Ashley set down Applet and reached out her hand, but it was three feet short. "Bend down."

If this is what it takes... Austin locked his hands on his knees and did his human stepladder routine.

"Oh!" he grunted as Ashley planted first one shoe squarely on his back, then the other. "Hurry it up."

The things he did for his sister! Austin wobbled, ready to drop her.

"Almost!" she called down.

He wondered what was taking so long. What if his sister still couldn't reach the link? Oh man, he was going to be hunched over for life. Either that or they were going to be stuck on this site forever with the Jolly Green Giant's bowling ball, just like poor Professor Braidwood.

"Got it!"

Ashley jumped down, and Austin grabbed the beagle for one more ride.

CHAPTER 14

Chicago Thumbnails

HONK!

It was *this* close. Ashley closed her eyes, waiting for the yellow taxi to plow into them and end it all. *Nice knowing you.* Good thing she knew she was going to heaven.

"Hey, sister!" The cabbie leaned out of his window and waved a hand at her. "You and your friend there wanna walk your dog on the sidewalk? Michigan Avenue here is for cars."

Michigan Avenue!

"Did you hear that, Austin?" She turned to her brother. "We made it to Michigan Avenue. This is Chicago."

Which meant they were just about a two-and-a-half-hour drive from home—or, at least, that would be true on the Outside, in the real world. This was only a virtual version of Chicago after all.

HONK-HONK!

"I said, move it!" yelled the cabbie. "I don't care how many arms you've lost. There's a war on, you know."

"Sorry!" Ashley dashed with her dazed brother and Applet to the side of the busy city street. Sure enough, Austin's arm had gone totally invisible almost all the way up to his shoulder. He wiggled his arm and slapped it with his good hand, the way somebody would if his arm was asleep.

Thankfully, this place looked pretty familiar, with Lake Michigan off to the right and the *Chicago Tribune* building towering up ahead. On either side, familiar Magnificent Mile department stores paraded up and down the avenue, and so did the people.

Only something wasn't quite right.

"Check it out." Austin pointed with his good arm, and his expression glassed over. "A 1935 Buick. I've only seen those in movies. And whoa—look over there. That's a Studebaker. What is this, an antique car museum site?"

Not quite. But the connection was plain: The professor had told them he earned his degree from the University of Chicago in 1943. They had linked to Chicago all right, but there was just one tiny problem. This was Chicago, *1943*. Not exactly the Saturday they'd left Normal.

Finding the right link home in the middle of all these people wasn't going to be easy. And even if they *did* find a link back to Normal, well, they still wouldn't really *be* in Normal, would they?

Oh brother.

Ashley whistled. "Look at all these links…" Words spilled all over the sidewalk to the point where it was hard not to step on one.

"Links, miss?" a young guy called to her from behind a steaming hot-dog wagon with a red-and-white-striped umbrella. "We've got links even internauts like you will love. Genuine Chicago hot dogs."

"Oh, not that kind of link." She smiled, but Austin drifted closer.

"I'm starving." He dropped a quarter into the guy's hand.

"What kinda funny money is this?" asked the young man, his expression turning as sour as sauerkraut. "I'm calling the cops!"

"No, it's okay." Ashley stepped in and pulled her brother way. "He's from…"

She was about to say Mexico—or anywhere else that might have given them a good excuse. But then she remembered Frank's bitter fudge and the bad taste it had left in her mouth. *Lies turn bitter.*

"He's not from around here," she finally said, and that was the truth. "He didn't mean anything by it."

"Hmmm." The hot-dog seller didn't quite look convinced,

but he flipped the quarter back at Austin, who caught it in his good hand.

"Come on." What would her brother do without her to rescue him? They kept walking down Michigan Avenue, trying to avoid all the sailors and shoppers and trying to keep Austin's arm hidden and Applet from sniffing everyone.

"Oh, how sweet." A woman in a fancy pink hat and white gloves stooped down to pet the beagle. "I always wondered if internauts had dogs too."

But then she caught sight of Austin. She looked at him just as Professor Braidwood had, as though he had a terrible disease. Without another word she straightened up and hurried off. She left Austin shaking his invisible arm. It seemed to have fallen asleep.

"It's still there," Ashley said. "Isn't it?"

But his face had turned white.

"Ashley, it's going really weird."

"Don't worry about it. We'll have it fixed up when we get home."

"No, you don't understand." He kept squeezing where his arm should have been, like a bodybuilder might flex his muscle. "Sometimes I feel it. And other times I don't feel a *thing*."

A couple of sailors in their white summer uniforms gave them a sideways look and steered out of the way as they walked past.

"Shh. Don't sweat it," she told him. "We'll—"

"What do you mean, don't sweat it? My hand disappears, then my arm, and now it's like they're not there anymore, and it's getting worse. How can you tell me not to sweat it? Maybe I really have caught some bad code and my program is being erased. The way it's going, there's not going to be much left of me in an hour or two."

"I hear you. But we're not going to fix anything standing here. Help me find a link we can use."

"Okay." Austin started walking again.

"How about *More Chicago History?*" Ashley asked as they hustled down the busy sidewalk. She passed her foot over the link, not touching it, and a black-and-white picture of a horse and carriage popped up in front of them.

"Hey, that's cool." Of course, even now that sort of thing would catch Austin's attention. "Thumbnails."

That would be *thumbnails,* as in small pictures, not *thumbnails,* as in the fingernails on thumbs. But thumbnails were great because for once they could check out a link without actually going through the hassle of jumping into it. They stopped to check out a thumbnail on the Great Chicago Fire.

"Let's not go there." Austin moved his foot over another link, something about how the Sears department store was started.

Ashley noticed she could see the link through her brother's foot.

"Here's *www-dot-FamousChicagoans-dot-org.*" Ashley did some searching of her own. "Al Capone, the gangster. Frank Lloyd Wright, the architect. Benny Goodman, the big-band leader. Oscar Mayer, the hot-dog maker. And then there's D. L. Moody."

"No kidding?" Mr. History Trivia King Austin moved in for a better look. "Dwight Lyman Moody. Born February 5, 1837. Died December 22, 1899. One of the greatest evangelists of his time. Helped start the Moody Bible Institute, along with—"

"Out of the way, internauts!" a woman bellowed behind them, and Ashley stepped to the side. Even so, the woman bumped into them from behind, sending them sprawling. Most people back in Normal didn't act like human bumper cars. But then again, this wasn't Normal. This was…

"Yikes!" Ashley couldn't keep her balance, and she grabbed for Austin's invisible arm. Unfortunately, her hand just swiped through where she thought his arm should have been…which meant she stumbled onto a link she really hadn't wanted to stumble on.

Here we go again!

CHAPTER 15

Moody Chat Room

"Sorry." Austin looked up from a stack of wooden folding chairs. "Didn't mean to drop in on you like this."

Everybody around him was singing, "Lose all their guilty stain, lose all their guilty stain…"

It sounded like an old hymn, and these folks at *www.Chicagochurchhistory.org* were belting it out as they followed a song leader up front, who was waving both hands like crazy. Austin was glad the singing crowd had pretty well drowned out the racket of his landing. There had to be hundreds of people in the large auditorium.

"You okay?" Ashley whispered into his ear from the seat beside him. *Good, she'd made it too.* Once again Applet was tucked under her arm, and nobody even seemed to care. At least they were all present and accounted for.

The people standing around Austin reached down and

hauled him up, as if they were used to people stumbling in off the street all the time. No big deal. They helped him to his feet, gave him a pat on the back, and kept right on singing.

Good thing he remembered to offer them his good arm, though, or he probably would have weirded them out.

"And sinners washed beneath that flood…"

The rafters in the big, wooden building were shaking from the sound. The simple oil-light chandeliers hanging from the ceiling swayed from side to side as they flickered with a cheery golden glow. A stocky, bearded man up on the front platform swayed along with them. A list of menu options hovered just above his head like a see-through poster. It was hard to tell what the list said from this far away, but Austin could make out two items on the menu: *His Early Days as a Shoe Salesman* and *The Sunday-School Ministry Grows.*

"That's him." Austin pointed.

"Who?" It seemed that Ashley didn't quite follow.

"The famous Chicagoan we linked to." He held up his finger the way he did when he came up with a winning answer in a Chiddix Junior High Knowledge Bowl competition. Sure, sometimes it took him a couple of minutes, but eventually he always came up with the right answer. "D. L. Moody. Maybe in the late 1800s."

The big man up front raised his hands just as the last

chorus finished. Everyone hushed to listen as the man spoke. His voice boomed and echoed even without a microphone.

"Don't forget my challenge to you this week," he reminded them, and many in the crowd nodded. "Look at yourself honestly. Ask the Lord where you stand with Him. And come back next week here to Farwell Hall with a decision."

The song leader stepped up one more time, song book ready. He had a menu over his head too, only it wasn't quite as long as Mr. Moody's.

Moody raised his hand. "And please don't forget the women's Bible study this Tuesday afternoon, led by our very own Emeline...Emma Dryer. Stand up, Miss Dryer, would you, please, so everyone can see you?"

A shy-looking, thirty-something woman in the second row stood up and waved her hand, though not very high—the way people do when they're embarrassed that everyone is staring at them. She had her own menu too, and a pretty long one at that. It listed things like *Her Role as a Christian Teacher* and *Her Part in Founding Moody Bible Institute*.

But Mr. Moody wasn't done calling attention to her.

"God has blessed Miss Dryer's ministry here ever since she gave up her position as head of the women's faculty at Illinois State Normal University. And now our last song, Ira?"

Moody didn't mean the university was normal, as in "not weird." A *normal* school was what people used to call places that trained teachers, which was how Normal, Illinois, got its name.

Austin didn't even hear the song leader announce the name of the closing hymn. "Did somebody say Illinois State Normal University?"

He turned to Ashley, hopping up and down. "I can't believe it. Normal! She's from Normal! Emma Dryer's our link home!"

"Cool it, Austin." Ashley tried to keep him on the floor as the people around them started singing again. "I heard."

"We can't lose her. No matter what happens! When this song's over, we push through the crowd and get to her links. Got it?"

Ashley nodded, but something strange was happening. The song leader had slowly lowered his hands, and the singers' voices were fading out, one by one, replaced by church bells and shouting, fire bells and more shouting, all outside. A boy ran to a window to look out as the singing turned to a worried murmur, something like the sound of five hundred people all whispering "uh-oh" at the same time.

A door to the street burst open.

"Listen to me!" announced a man. He wore a dark uniform and a peaked red-and-black cap. "Whatever you do, don't panic. The fire is still a few miles away. But we need to get everyone out of this building as quickly as possible."

The whispered "uh-ohs" turned to mumbled "oh-noes" as the fireman explained what he wanted them to do and what was happening outside.

"The city of Chicago is burning!"

CHAPTER 16

Web Jamming

So Ashley and Austin had managed to land themselves in the middle of the Great Chicago Fire of 1871.

The good news: Nobody in the crowded auditorium panicked. Mr. Moody prayed for a moment before the group dismissed, and he seemed calm enough. And even though Ashley could see the tight expressions on everyone's faces, no one was pushing or shoving to leave.

The bad news: This crowd was moving toward three main exit doors behind her and Austin. For the Websters, it was something like standing in front of Niagara Falls, only without the Niagara and without any falls. In the flow of people, they had lost sight of Emma Dryer, their possible link home.

Ashley kept a tight grip on Applet to keep the poor dog from being crushed. As it was, the beagle rested her paws on a short woman's shoulders. The woman turned and gave them a surprised look. Obviously, she wasn't used to having animals lick her ear.

"Sorry." Ashley apologized and did her best to move against the crowd toward where Emma Dryer had been, but she felt like a salmon swimming upstream.

"Coming through!" yelled Austin. A lot of good that did. Who did he think he was, Moses parting the Red Sea?

Well, the crowd wasn't parting, and Ashley thought she might have to do something drastic, like shout, "I'm going to be sick!" It had worked once before. But even if it were true, she didn't think it would do any good, though the pressing in of the crowd *was* making her a little woozy, come to think of it. Right now she could faint and not even hit the floor. But that wouldn't help them find Emma Dryer.

"She was in the second row," Ashley shouted to her brother. The noise of the crowd was growing. "I don't know if she's coming this way."

Ashley thought Miss Dryer had to come this way eventually if she wanted to leave the building, and that was all there was to it. Meanwhile, moms and dads were calling for their children, and a few younger kids started crying. Ashley couldn't blame them; she was almost ready to join in. *Mommy!*

Mommy wasn't there, of course, but Ashley finally caught sight of the next best thing floating just above the crowd.

"See it, Austin?" She grabbed her brother's arm and pointed. "Miss Dryer's menu."

"Her Work with the Chicago Women's Aid Society," read her brother. *"Her Early Bible Study Programs."*

There was much more to the list—and it was definitely all about Emma Dryer. Only problem was, a crowd at least twenty or thirty people thick separated Emma Dryer and her links from where they stood. And they were drifting backward, the wrong way. Emma was slipping out the side.

There was nothing else to do. "Miss Dryer!" Ashley shouted, and Austin jumped and waved.

That's when somebody noticed his arms. By this time his left arm was totally gone, and now his right arm was fuzzy and see-through from the elbow to the shoulder. It seemed as if Austin's hand and wrist were floating on their own.

"He's erasing!" shrieked a woman.

The news of the raging fire outside was nothing compared to the effect Austin was having on the crowd.

"No!" a little boy wailed. "No!"

"Aai-EEEE!"

Ashley could understand why everyone was going berserk. Having Austin in the auditorium was like telling guppies to stay cool about the new fish being dumped into their bowl. Hey, come on, kids. It's just a piranha.

Ashley never did figure out how everybody was able to scramble away from them so quickly. Hadn't they been packed into the auditorium pretty good? Maybe their files were compressing, squishing down until they took up hardly any space.

Anyway, no one was going to get within ten feet of poor Austin. And he didn't make things any better when he raised his hands—at least it looked to Ashley as if that's what he was trying to do—to calm everybody down.

"I'm just an internaut, folks," he told them. "We're here to see Miss Dryer. And you can't catch this bad code from me."

Everybody stared at him as if he were reading the news in Russian.

"At least, I don't *think* you can."

Oh brother. Ashley closed her eyes. *Time to go.* But the panic had helped to clear things out well enough so Ashley could almost reach up and click on Miss Dryer's link—the one that said *Her Time at Illinois State Normal University.* The pleasant-looking woman was actually working her way through the remaining people to them.

"Oh!" Ashley wasn't quite sure what to say. "I'm awfully sorry, Miss Dryer. My brother doesn't mean to scare anyone. We just…"

"Let's keep moving," she told them, looking toward the doors. "Tell me who you are and why you're here."

Ashley could see the menu of links hovering just above the

woman's head like a kite on a short string. If she could just reach them...

"It's your links!" Austin blurted out, trying to point. By this time only the fingertips on his right hand were left, and he looked like something out of a sci-fi film.

"Oh." Miss Dryer lifted her eyes for a moment. "Sometimes I forget they're there."

"We need to touch one of them to get home." Ashley wanted to just stand up on a chair and reach up for the link the way she'd done back in the tunnel. "We're from Normal too."

"I see." Miss Dryer looked from Austin to Ashley, her eyes showing concern. "Then you'd better go there and get your friend some help very soon. I'm afraid he's not going to last much longer."

CHAPTER 17

Bad Code

🖱

"Miss Dryer is right." Austin looked up from peeking down inside his T-shirt. "I'm not going to last much longer."

"Oh, come on." Ashley couldn't believe he was giving up so easily. "I thought you always wanted to be invisible so you could sneak around."

"You don't get it." He nodded down at his left arm. "At first it was just see-through, like ice. But then it started to tingle and go totally invisible. Now I can barely feel it. Here, try to grab it."

Ashley tried and missed. Nothing there! *Uh-oh.*

Austin ignored Applet when she wagged her tail at him.

"There, see? It's spreading. Like I'm a leper."

"Don't be gross. You're not a leper. You don't have a disease."

"Oh really? What do you call this? My left arm is almost gone, and the right one's on its way. My legs are fading fast. I can still walk on 'em, but for how long? Even my chest is see-through. What's next? I'm erasing like those people in Chicago said."

"Well, we're back in Normal now. We'll get somebody to rewrite your code if that's what it takes."

"Who? Ms. Blankenskrean? She has an office downtown, you know."

"No!" Ashley didn't want to run into that woman again, though she still wished the PDA were in safer hands.

"Well, we aren't home yet, Ashley. This is just a digital copy of downtown Normal. The chamber of commerce probably did some quick scans for their Web site. I don't even see any people here. Do you? I'm just going to fade into nothing here on this low-budget site, and there's nothing you or I can do about it. In fact—"

"In fact nothing," Ashley snapped as she paced in front of the fancy old Normal Theater, one of her favorite places in the whole world. What was Austin talking about? This was home; it sure looked like it anyway. They could get help here. "What about Aunt Jessi? She might be able to do something."

"Yeah, what about her?" Austin slumped down to sit on the sidewalk. "I was hoping she would have found us by now."

Right across the street stood the brick post office. A couple doors down was the University Christian Church, a nice sandstone-brick building that anchored that corner of North Street.

Everything was where it was supposed to be.

"Maybe we should try to go back to our house," she thought aloud.

Austin shook his head.

"Do you have any better ideas?" she asked.

"You go ahead." He hung his head. "I'll wait here for you. Of course, if you just find a pile of clothes when you get back, you'll know I'm already gone."

"Stop it!" Austin was really over the line now. Her brother couldn't just disappear forever, could he? She would show him. She started down the street. "You're not going to give up, and I'm not either. We can get help. In fact, look. I'll go down to this church and—"

Ka-BOING!

Ashley bounced off an unseen barrier and fell backward to the sidewalk.

"What in the world?" she rubbed her nose and tried to figure out what she had just walked into. It reminded her of the time she had slammed face first into the closed sliding-glass patio door at their home when she was five.

Austin looked up with a dead-tired look on his face; she felt the same way. Slowly his expression melted into a smile.

"It's a computer screen, Ashley." Well, at least her clown act had brought Austin back to his feet. "You just ran into a screen!"

"And that was good?" Ashley wasn't sure why it was such a big deal, except that they had never come up against the inside of a computer screen before. She shuffled up again—slowly this time and sideways—to see what she could see.

"This is very cool." Austin hobbled up next to her. He really was not looking good, but Ashley wasn't going to tell him that. They both leaned as close to the screen as they could, and Ashley nearly lost it when she finally saw through to the other side.

"Lookit, lookit, lookit!" She knocked on the inside of the glass screen, then pounded. "It's the library out there!"

And not just any library. They stared out through the screen at the Normal Public Library—the real thing, not an Internet copy. Ashley could see the real live reference librarian, a sweet lady named Mrs. Freeman, walk by with a stack of magazines.

"We must be looking out through one of those computer terminals set up between the reference desk and the kids' section." Austin's eyes were wide; he looked as if he couldn't believe it either. "I was just here last week looking for bird books."

It felt terrific to see the real world again, but it didn't exactly help them get out from inside the World Wide Web.

"Hey, Mrs. Freeman!" Ashley pounded until her knuckles throbbed. Their favorite librarian smiled and waved at a girl on her way out.

"This is worse than worse." Austin groaned. "We're so close!"

Ashley kicked at the screen. What would it take to break it? And what would happen if they did?

She slammed at the screen with her fists, then rammed it with her shoulder. *Ow.* No one seemed to notice. The girl nearest them lifted her books from the counter and walked right on by.

The Websters gave up and stared, their jaws hanging.

"Aw, come on." Ashley didn't even try to hold back her tears. She looked over at her brother—or what was left of him. Austin was right: They were no closer to home now than they had been back in the Volkswagen factory, hiding from Ms. Blankenskrean.

CHAPTER 18

Home but Not

This was where the cavalry was supposed to come riding to the rescue. Where the bad guy was supposed to turn into the good guy. Where Ashley was supposed to wake up to find out that it was all just a bad dream, like Dorothy had discovered in *The Wizard of Oz.*

Well, we're still a long way from Kansas, Toto—or Applet. Sorry. And Ashley knew from Mr. Little's English class that those were pretty bad ways to end a story. Besides, it wasn't time to end the Websters' story just yet. No matter how much of her brother had disappeared, she wasn't going to let Austin give up either. She motioned for him to follow her.

"You don't really think she'll be glad to see us, do you?" Austin shuffled his feet along the downtown sidewalk. Well, what was left of his feet. His shoes and his clothes draped a nearly invisible body. Actually, even the clothes were starting to fade away.

"No," Ashley admitted. "But what other choice do we have? She'll know a way to get back."

"You're forgetting that she left us online on purpose. She'll do the same thing again—if she's even here. She won't care."

Ashley knew her brother was right. But what else could they do? Austin was going to be one hundred percent erased pretty soon, not just invisible. Would Ashley be able to get him back after that?

Don't think about it. She slowed as they neared the door of the NCCC office in the neat, two-story brick building. The gold letters on a cheery green door read "Normal Council on Civil Correctness." That sounded pleasant enough—until Ashley thought about it. What exactly was "civil correctness" anyway?

They mounted a short stairway to the second-floor entry to find out, with Applet tapping along behind them.

"I hear her!" whispered Austin. If the murmuring voice on the other side of the door was anyone's, it was Mattie Blanken-skrean's. The woman laughed as if someone had told a joke on the other end of a phone conversation. Yeah, it was Ms. B all right.

They both pressed their ears against the door. At first they didn't hear much of interest, only stuff about budgets and audit reports and meetings with the board of directors. *Bo-ring.*

Ashley yawned. She was about to give up and knock on the door when the conversation turned.

"Oh, all right," Ms. B sighed. "I was hoping not to be disturbed for a while so I could get some work done here. But if you really need me back in Normal, well…"

Ashley and Austin looked at each other. "Back" in Normal?

"Check your e-mail in three minutes," she continued. "I'll be there. Don't keep me waiting."

"This we have *got* to see," Ashley whispered to her brother before turning to run back down the stairs.

They both knew they wouldn't see anything if they were standing outside the closed office door. Outside at the back of the building they could see that the NCCC office had windows, but they were a good eight feet off the ground. Only one thing to do.

"Don't fall!" Ashley warned as her brother climbed on her shoulders. The nearly invisible Austin had lost so many pounds it was ridiculous. A minute later Ashley felt for his see-through shoes—she was relieved there was still something to feel—and she stood up as straight as she could, doing her best not to let him fall. She felt as if she were balancing a marshmallow statue, only without the marshmallow and without the statue.

"What do you see?" she hissed.

"Wait a minute." He would have to hurry up. "Whoa!"

"Shh!" Ashley whispered. "Don't let her hear you."

"She just put her head down on a scanner and scanned it," he said. "Which is either very cool or very weird."

Ashley wasn't sure which either.

"What now?" she asked.

"Now she's going over to her computer."

"For what?"

"Can't really tell. Looks like a mail program. She's typing something in."

"Do you think she's really—?" Ashley wondered aloud as Austin caught his breath.

"You won't believe this."

"Come on, Austin. After what we've been through, what wouldn't I believe?"

A few seconds ticked by, but they felt like minutes. At last he looked down and grinned. Or at least it looked as if Austin was grinning. Even his face was mostly see-through by now, including his glasses.

"I think she just e-mailed herself."

"No way. Are you sure?"

Austin hopped down. "No, I'm not sure. All I know is she's not up there anymore."

"This is too weird." Ashley tried to think fast, but none of this made any sense at all. "So does she just show up—*bing!*— in somebody's in box?"

"Yeah, like, 'You've got mail.' "

There wasn't much left of Austin, but at least what was left still had a shred of humor.

"Come on. Let's try it then."

Being a burglar wasn't as hard as Ashley thought. The second-story main door was locked, but a first-story window wasn't, and they and Applet connected to Ms. B's office through an inside stairwell.

"Piece of cake." Ashley stood in the office with her hands on her hips. "Was it that computer over there?"

Austin didn't have a chance to answer. And considering the fact that, other than Ms. B, they hadn't met anyone else on this Web site, the *BAAA-BAAA-BAAA* of the security alarm seemed a little over the top.

"Why didn't you tell me she set an alarm?" Ashley yelled, her fingers in her ears. Applet seemed to howl her agreement.

But the *BAAA-BAAA-BAAA* shut off just like that. The alarm echoed in her ears even after it stopped.

Someone answered from behind her, but it didn't sound like Austin. "I *said* he didn't tell you because he could not have known."

Ashley didn't have to turn around to know who was standing right behind her.

Ms. Mattie Blankenskrean.

CHAPTER 19

AshLey@NormaL.com

"I have a door, you know." Ms. Blankenskrean's voice frosted the back of Ashley's neck. "You could have knocked."

"Would you have let us in and helped us?" Ashley asked, trying very hard to be brave.

"Knowing what I know about you two…" A pause. A laugh. "I'm really not sure. But I have to give you credit. You're a lot more resourceful than I thought, coming all this way."

"All we wanted was to get back home."

"Of course." Another laugh. "That and to sabotage my work, isn't that right? They're still trying to fix my PDA Outside in the *real* Normal. In the meantime I'm using this office for a little peace and…well, never mind. What you don't know won't hurt you. Let's talk about you for a change. I imagine your parents will soon become quite worried about you. And I don't believe anyone is going to believe a word of what that poor cousin of yours is going to tell them."

"That would be my aunt."

"Oh no, dear. She's only just your age. In any case, I do feel sorry for what's about to happen to her. Poor little...Jessica, is it?"

"What do you know about Jessi?"

"Only what my staff has told me from the time I first met you. We monitor the online situation, you know. Keep track."

Ms. B glanced under her desk.

"Where's your brother, by the way? I hope he didn't steal anything from the office."

Ashley wasn't sure if she owed Ms. Blankenskrean the truth—or anything else. Her first thought was to say nothing, but something made Ashley decide to turn and face the woman head on.

"Austin wouldn't steal a thing." Ashley felt her face turn red. "And he's..."

That's when she noticed the shimmering clothes on the floor in the corner, a see-through pile that started with Austin's Nikes and worked itself up to his Chargers T-shirt. It reminded her of the hat and carrot on their front lawn last February after a thaw had melted the snowman they'd built. It was as if Austin had just melted away.

"Speak up. Where is he hiding?"

By this time Ashley couldn't see through her tears. What did getting home matter now?

Austin was gone.

"He's not here," Ashley finally forced it out. "Not anymore."

Applet growled quietly as the woman sneered down at them.

"Somehow I have a hard time believing you. And you'll have to take your animal outside. Don't want any hairs or messes on the carpet, even if this *is* a Web site."

Ms. B aimed her foot at Applet, who was not about to let herself be kicked. The beagle must have been waiting for an excuse to lock her teeth onto some piece of Mattie Blankenskrean.

"Beast!" She danced on one foot and dangled the still-biting Applet above the floor from the other. "I'll have you erased so fast—"

"No, you won't!"

Maybe the word *erased* set Ashley off, or maybe she'd just had enough of Ms. B. In any case, she wasn't going to let Ms. B erase anything. Ashley tackled the woman, taking her to the floor with a grunt and a shout.

It was a lot like a catfight, only without the cats. But not without the fight. And goodness, it seemed as if somebody else was helping out too. Because after about ten seconds, Ms. B gave up, her arms falling to her sides.

"Let go of me!" she begged.

Suddenly, Ashley's hotheaded anger drained away. Where

had it come from anyway? *How embarrassing.* She caught her breath, straightened her shirt, and stood back up.

"I'm sorry." She held out her hand. "Maybe I shouldn't have done that, but—"

"I'll say you shouldn't have." Ms. B tried to rise but only wriggled on the floor like a caterpillar that had been taped to a science display. Two white-gloved hand icons held her down, one on her right shoulder and the other on her left leg. Where had they come from?

PLINK-PLINK-PLINK!

Ashley had to look twice to see where the plinking noise was coming from. And when she saw the huge face and nose staring at her from just outside the office windows, she nearly joined Ms. B on the floor.

"Austin!" She took a step closer. "What are you doing out there?"

"I knew it!" Ms. B was clearly not a happy camper. "I knew your brother was hiding."

"He's not hiding." Ashley smiled. "He's on the other side."

Sure enough, Austin *was* on the Outside, looking in at them through a computer screen and plinking his finger on the glass.

Ashley pointed to his pile of clothes. Boys never pick up after themselves.

"Sorry about the mess," he said. "I'll pick them up."

"But how…?" Ashley wanted to know.

"I sneaked out of there while you guys were arguing and e-mailed myself home. Had to take the clothes off or people would have seen me—at least what was left of me."

Ashley cleared her throat. *Oh brother!*

"I didn't mean to leave you behind," he added, "but I thought I'd better get out before I totally disappeared."

Ms. B groaned, but a third hand icon now covered her mouth. Where had they all come from?

"You're okay now?" Ashley asked.

"Yeah, like new. And I found some clothes in a hurry. You just need to do the same thing. I mean, use Ms. B's e-mail station. I don't know how long I can keep her pinned down."

PLINK-PLINK-PLINK!

This time another face appeared on yet another screen, off to the other side. It was the oddest thing. Ashley wasn't sure how many people could be watching her at once, but she felt as if she were standing between two mirrors in a department store and seeing herself a thousand times over.

"Where have you been, Ash?"

Ashley had to laugh at the sound of her aunt Jessi's voice. Where had *she* been? She and Austin would have to teach Jessi a thing or two about Web searches as soon as she got back. Jessi's aunt peeked in at her and Applet, and Ashley waved back at the screen.

"I've been right here, Jessi. But I'm ready to—"

She was going to say, "Ready to come home now," but Ms. B groaned again. Ashley looked down and wondered what to do. Leave her and run? Help her? At least the three hand icons were holding her for now. She couldn't budge.

"Come on, Ash," said her aunt. "We can't hold her much longer."

"Coming!"

That explained all the hand icons: Jessi *and* Austin had come to the rescue—Jessie from her house, and Austin from his laptop. But Ashley didn't have time to try to figure out where Ms. B would go once they freed her. She quickly ran with Applet over to the scanner, worked it the way Austin had told her, attached herself and the beagle to the e-mail, and held her breath. Maybe they'd get the champion beagle back home after all. This was a piece of cake.

Or at least it was a piece of cake as long as you remembered to send yourself to the right e-mail address.

"Uh-oh," she told herself as, too late, she realized her mistake. Ashley wondered whose in box she and Applet might find themselves in and on which computer in which country.

She braced herself for another adventure.

To be continued…

The HyperLinkz Guide to Safe Surfing

Hey, Austin T. Webster here. Since Ashley hogged a lot of the *Fudge Factor* action, I get to do the guide this time. You'll find out what happens to her and Applet in the third Hyperlinkz book, which is called (drumroll, please) *Web Jam.*

Okay, enough about the next book. I really want to tell you more about the characters and places found on some of the cool Web sites we visited.

Let's start with Brother Andrew or Andrew van der Bijl, which is his real name. You can read all about him on the Internet, or you can check out his famous book called *God's Smuggler.* Try typing "Brother Andrew" into a search engine; you'll be amazed at all the amazing adventures he had smuggling God's Word to people who never had a Bible of their own. You might even find a photo of his old, blue Volkswagen.

Today, a lot more people have taken on Brother Andrew's work, delivering Bibles to people in countries where freedom of religion isn't allowed. There are still too many places like that. To find out more, check out *www.opendoorsusa.org.*

Unlike *www.opendoorsusa.org,* which is a real Web site,

some of the sites Ashley and I visited were made up for the story, so you can't always visit the *same* places we did. But one site you can visit is *www.heroesofhistory.com.* That is where you can find out about people like Corrie ten Boom and George Washington Carver and Mother Teresa. Try *www.christian heroes.com,* too.

Ashley: And Emeline Dryer! Don't forget to mention Emeline Dryer.

Austin: I wasn't going to forget her. It's just that Miss Dryer isn't on that list. In fact, you'd probably never heard of her until you read about how my sister and I met her in this story. Well, that's probably the way she would have wanted it. Because Emeline Dryer—her friends called her Emma—was never really in the spotlight. The closest she came to it was a couple of years in the late 1860s when she was named the preceptress of the teacher's college in my hometown of Normal, Illinois. *(Preceptress* is just an old way of saying *woman principal.)* That was actually a pretty important job, and it put her name in the history books. But she gave up good money and a good job to go to Chicago to work for nothing in a ministry she cared about. And that's where God used her. With her background and gift for Bible teaching, she was one of the key people who started the Moody Bible Institute. Today, the Moody Bible Institute is still a great Bible college where thousands of people have been trained for Christian service. (And here's a bit of trivia: The guys who live in Dryer Hall, a dormitory on the Moody campus, are still called "Emma's boys.")

I haven't mentioned D. L. Moody himself yet, but the founder of Moody Bible Institute was one of the most important preachers of his time. I could go on and on about him, but I'll leave it to you to discover more.

Ashley: You skipped over Corrie ten Boom and Rahab.

Austin: Not on purpose. I was just getting to those two. First Corrie ten Boom. Like Brother Andrew, she also wrote a famous book. Hers is called *The Hiding Place,* and it's a great read. You can find out more about Corrie ten Boom online, too. Most of the time she's mentioned for helping hide Jewish people in Holland during World War II. They have even planted a special tree at the Yad Vashem Memorial in Israel to honor her because she did the right thing.

Corrie ten Boom is also remembered for lying to the Nazis when they came looking for the Jews who were hiding in the ten Boom home. When asked, Corrie told them, "No Jews here."

I wonder what I would have done in Corrie ten Boom's place. All I can say is that Corrie ten Boom never bragged about lying, but I think she believed it would have been more wrong to let innocent people die. God knew her heart, and it all comes down to grace.

Ashley: Preach it, Brother Austin.

Austin: Hey, I'm just getting warmed up. The same goes

for Rahab, who played only a small part in the Old Testament story of how the Israelites came to their land. Of course she helped them, but the real story about Rahab is how she's mentioned not once in the New Testament, not twice, but *three* times. And each time she's described as a hero.

First, there's Matthew 1:5, which says, "Salmon the father of Boaz, whose mother was Rahab, Boaz the father of Obed, whose mother was Ruth, Obed the father of Jesse…"

Now I don't know what you think, but I think it's very cool to be mentioned in the list of Jesus's ancestors.

Then there's Hebrews 11:31. "By faith the prostitute Rahab, because she welcomed the spies, was not killed with those who were disobedient."

It's pretty cool to be patted on the back in the Faith Heroes Hall of Fame.

And finally look at James 2:25, where it reads, "In the same way, was not even Rahab the prostitute considered righteous for what she did when she gave lodging to the spies and sent them off in a different direction?"

Wait a minute. *Righteous?* As in she did the right thing? A lot of people argue the point, but Rahab saw the big picture, and she did what she could to protect God's people. She was probably a little rough around the edges, but like Corrie ten Boom, she wanted to do the right thing, and God used her.

Well, that about does it, except for a couple more facts:

Dr. Braidwood actually was a famous archaeologist at the University of Chicago, and many people say that he really did inspire the popular *Indiana Jones* movies. The Germans really did invent the Volkswagen as a "people's car" right before World War II. The town of Normal, Illinois, really does have a university—one that started as a college to train teachers (a "normal" school). You can find out about all that on the Web, but don't believe it just because it's there. Dig deeper to find the truth.

Oh yeah—and don't forget to join us in *Web Jam* to find out what's happened to Ashley.

Ashley: I'm fine, really.

Austin: We'll see about that.

See ya,
Austin (and Ashley)

P.S. to parents: The Internet can be a lot of fun, but please make sure your child is surfing safely. That means being there for them. Know what they're accessing. And consider using a good filtering service or software; it can help you sidestep some nasty surprises. While we can't tell you which filter is best for your family's needs, you might begin by checking out a great site called *www.filterreview.com*. It will give you many of the options so that you can make a wise decision.

Please visit Robert Elmer's Web site at *www.RobertElmerBooks.com* to learn more about other books he's written or to schedule him to speak to your school or home-school group.